A Spirit in the Dark
A DCI Luke Wiley Book

Jaye Bailey

A SPIRIT IN THE DARK
Published Worldwide by Two Yards Crime.
This edition published in 2024.

Copyright © 2024 by Jaye Bailey
The right of Jaye Bailey to be identified as the author of this work has been asserted in accordance with the Copyright, Design and Patents Act 1988.

All rights reserved. No part of this book may be reproduced in any form or by any electronic or mechanical means, including information storage and retrieval systems, without written permission from the author, except for the use of brief quotations in a book review.

All characters and events in this book are entirely fictional. Any references to historical events, real people, or real locales are used fictitiously. Other names, characters, places, and incidents are the product of the author's imagination, and any resemblance to actual events or locales or persons, living or dead, is entirely coincidental.

1.1.1

Also by Jaye Bailey

The DCI Luke Wiley Thrillers

A Grave Return

The Quiet and the Dead

The Killing Pages

A Spirit in the Dark

Hidden Demons

Prologue

For the first time in many weeks, she had a Friday evening with no plans. She wasn't quite sure what to do with herself.

Kicking off her shoes as she entered her flat, she nudged the light switch up with her elbow, as one hand was carrying her laptop bag and the other, a tote bag full of spontaneous shopping from the delicatessen next to the tube station. As she had exited the station and begun walking towards her flat, she had stopped abruptly, turned around and popped back inside the deli.

What she did not have in her flat, she had thought, was wine.

While she was in the deli, she kept spying items that she fancied. Some olives, fennel salami, a gorgeous looking salted flatbread. As she was going to be alone on a Friday night for the first time in ages, why not make herself a beautiful little supper of moreish things she could eat with her fingers, and pour herself a nice glass of wine.

It sounded perfect.

The flat was cold and while she loved the space, because it was on the ground floor of what was a three storey house before it was sectioned off into two separate dwellings, it often felt damp.

Spring was a little late arriving in London this year, and although the snowdrops had already sprouted, bloomed, and faded and daffodils were now dotted around all of the city's green spaces, it was still chilly. Easter weekend was only two weeks away and there were still rumours of snow.

When she had come to view this flat she fell in love with it immediately. She had just turned twenty eight and finally had enough income to move out of her flat share into her own space. She would probably have been thrilled wherever she ended up, but this flat in particular was charming. The rooms were a bit basic, but the entire flat was painted a warm maple colour and a large open plan living and dining room led out to a flagstone patio. The entire back wall of the space was glass and had a cleverly installed door that your eye wasn't immediately drawn to, so it felt like a hidden entranceway to the patio and beautifully cultivated garden beyond it.

The friend who had accompanied her on the viewing remarked that this wasn't going to work. The friend had laughed and pointed out that she tended to jump at every little thing, and there was no way she was going to feel comfortable living in a glass fishbowl like this on her own.

Her friend had a point. She didn't like the annoyance of living with flatmates, but she was grateful for the security that it brought. She did jump at any noise she couldn't identify and she did have the tendency to think a burglar was always prowling just outside. She blamed this anxiety on scary movies she watched at an age that was completely inappropriate, but these emotions get imprinted early and she knew that she would likely never shake off the feeling.

But she had the money to rent this flat and she could take

comfort in the fact that her garden was completely walled in on all sides with the neighbours' gardens surrounding it. She didn't back onto a lane or an empty car park or a cemetery that could hide a murderer.

And besides, the flat had a feature that she had long coveted. It had a real, proper fireplace. Not a wood burner, which you could still find occasionally in the boroughs of London that hadn't banned them due to air pollution, and where was the romance in a wood burner? They were big and bulky and even if they had a glass door, you couldn't hear the sizzle and the crack of burning wood. You couldn't smell the warmth and glow of the fire.

Gas fireplaces were lovely, and sure you could flick a switch and have it on or off with ease and at your leisure. But there wasn't much romance in that either.

Not that she was the kind of woman who needed romance in her life, but she had always dreamt of her own home in London, picking up wine and a few outrageously priced deli items, lighting a fire and relaxing with a glass and a book.

Tonight, she was going to make all of this happen, especially as she wasn't supposed to have had this Friday night free. She worked long hours as a publicist for a communications agency that specialized in restaurants and events. So if she wasn't stuck in the office, she was usually at a work event on a Friday evening, ensuring that everything was running smoothly and networking with anyone and everyone. It was fun, but it was exhausting.

A free Friday night was otherwise spent with friends. She wasn't especially outgoing or social when it came to her personal life, but she had forced herself to meet as many people as humanly possible when she moved to London from the blink-and-you'd-forget-it tiny town in the middle of the country where she grew up. And now seven years later, she had a warm and wonderful group of girlfriends who she wanted to see whenever her time allowed.

She hadn't seen any of them over the past month. She knew that her friends were probably a little bit irritated with her, and would very likely have a go at her when they next went out. She could hear them now.

You are the kind of girl who ignores her friends when she meets someone?

We've been dumped for your new boyfriend!

Who is he?

She was guilty of these things, and she felt even guiltier that she wasn't seeing her friends tonight. The thing is, she had been due to see the new guy.

He was really cute. A month into whatever this was, she was very into him. Could her friends blame her if when she had a free Friday night that she would rather see him?

Probably.

But for now she was going to just go with it.

She had been at a cocktail bar opening in East London and the bar's owner had been very demanding. Things weren't quite right; had so-and-so RSVPed; the plants he had requested were different from the ones they had installed over the bar; why weren't the servers wearing ties as had been requested?

After she had dealt with every issue thrown at her, she found herself stuck at the bar owner's side, being introduced to people she hoped never to see again, and she desperately wished that she had worn boots instead of heels. As she shifted from foot to foot trying to ease the pain in the balls of her feet by shifting her weight, she saw him.

He was staring right at her. It was as if he understood her discomfort, that every part of her didn't want to be there. He smiled and shook his head slightly. It was as if they were already in on a joke that no one else in the room thought was funny.

She smiled back at him and hoped the bar owner didn't notice that she shrugged her shoulders.

Suddenly he was walking towards her, his cocktail in one hand and the other gently touching the backs and arms of the people in the crowd he was maneuvering around. He wasn't very tall, but his body was well proportioned to his height and his trousers and slim collared shirt looked effortless on him.

She found herself involuntarily opening her mouth to speak as he approached, but she had no idea what to say to this stranger.

'It's you,' he said, and she was momentarily taken aback. Did she know him? Was he someone from a previous event and she couldn't place him?

'Hi,' she responded.

'My apologies for interrupting,' he said, nodding at the owner. 'But may I steal her away for just a moment?'

As she gratefully stepped away from the tedious conversation she had been mired within, she took a good look at him. He had sandy hair parted at the side, a bit of it flopping forward and tickling his eyelashes — he flipped his head back slightly in response, a cute mannerism that she would get to know over the next few weeks. His eyes looked kind, just beginning to crinkle at the edges and she guessed he was in his mid-thirties. He had a bit of stubble and when she looked a bit more closely, she could see that it was meant to hide a long, slightly raised white scar that ran from his top lip to just underneath his nose.

He would have had a cleft palate corrected as a child.

'You looked like you needed rescuing.'

'Thank you for coming to the rescue.'

'Anytime.'

He had waited for her all evening — even after all of the

guests had left the event and the caterers had packed up and the owner had finally signed the paperwork she needed him to sign — he sat on a bar stool reading the paper that he had procured from somewhere. Folding it carefully and placing it on the counter, he had swivelled towards her and jumped down.

'Are you exhausted, or can I now buy you a proper drink?'

He was so cute, and so attentive and they had seen each other at least twice a week for the past month. Her friends would understand when they finally met him.

On this particular Friday evening, they had originally been due to go out for dinner and maybe catch a film if something was playing a bit later that caught their interest. But he had called a couple of days ago to say that he had been spontaneously invited out of town on a skiing weekend with friends and did she mind if they re-scheduled.

She had been stung by the phone call. He didn't ask if she skied, or would fancy joining them. It felt very clear that she was not being included.

So instead of dusting herself off and texting a friend to arrange other plans, she decided to stay in and have a night on her own. Part of her didn't feel like explaining this guy and his behaviour just yet to her friends. She was sure that they would be sympathetic, but she didn't feel up to that kind of conversation.

The wine and expensive charcuterie and a roaring fire would do just fine.

As she turned on the lights and lowered the blinds that covered the giant glass wall and door that led to the garden, she couldn't help but shiver. She checked the lock on the patio door and jiggled the handle. It was securely locked. Of course it was — she had checked it before she left for the office that morning, just as she had checked it before she went to bed the previous night. It was always locked and she silently scolded herself for being so anxious about it.

She turned on the television to see if there were any good Friday night films about to begin, but the menu on the screen didn't reveal anything especially interesting. She left the tv on a channel that was playing re-runs of a sitcom she had seen a thousand times before, but it was a bit of company as she unwrapped the meats and olives and arranged them on a plate. They would warm up to room temperature while she took a quick shower to rinse off the long week at work.

She thought, for a moment, about lighting the fire before her shower. To step out of a shower and into a fresh pair of yoga leggings and a baggy sweatshirt with the fireplace already roaring and warm would be divine, not to mention how quickly it would deal with the damp air in the flat. But she was wary of an open flame that would be unattended, even for just five minutes, so she settled with laying the kindling, the twisted pieces of newspaper and a couple of very small, dry logs.

Just to be extra decadent, she decided to pour herself a glass of wine and take it with her into the bathroom. She tore the capsule over the neck of the bottle with her house keys, tossing the keys back onto the counter as the red wine was decanted into her glass. She inhaled the aroma in the glass and took a long drink.

The bathroom was small and with the door closed, it steamed up very quickly. She stepped into the tub and let the hot water pour over her and although she had washed her hair that morning, she decided to run conditioner through it again, using a detangling wet brush, which made her scalp tingle as she combed it across her head and through her hair.

She pulled the shower curtain back and reached towards the wine glass that was balanced next to the sink. As she picked it up, she heard something.

Was someone knocking on the door?

She stood very still and strained to hear over the sound of the shower. Everything seemed quiet, but she did not take a drink from the glass, deciding to rinse her hair and get out of the shower. She hated that she now had a sense of unease.

As she turned the shower knob to stop the flow of water, she heard it again.

A thud. Like someone had dropped something on the floor.

But she was alone in the flat.

For a split second, she thought of calling out to see who was there. But the only person who had keys to this flat was her landlord. And he would not let himself in unannounced on a Friday evening.

Although the shower had been steamy and hot, she was instantly cold and one giant shiver uncontrollably shook through her body. She tried to be as quiet as possible as she pulled back the shower curtain, its metal hooks scraping against the pole. Her feet squeaked on the ceramic surface of the bathtub as she lifted one foot out and onto the bathmat, and then the other.

Anyone in the flat would have heard the shower running. They would know she was in there.

She grabbed the bathrobe hanging on the hook on the back of the door and threw her arms into it, not bothering to towel dry first. She was aware of her wet hair dripping down her face and onto the nape of her neck.

Her phone.

Thank god she had brought her phone into the bathroom with her. It was lying next to her glass of red wine on the counter.

Should she call the police? And say what? She heard a noise in her flat and she doesn't want to come out of the bathroom?

Taking a deep breath, she quickly wrapped the discarded towel around her wet hair, tucking up the end so that it would stay affixed there, and she picked up her phone. Her other hand hovered over the door handle and she counted to three.

Easing it down, she winced at the click as it released its latch, and she pulled the door towards her.

The smell hit her instantly.

Burning wood.

Someone had lit the fire she had laid.

She did not wonder for even a split second if she was mistaken — that the smell was something else, or she had misremembered and had actually struck a match and lit the kindling before running the shower.

She knew she was in danger.

Through the crack in the door, she strained to look left and right and she saw no one. It would be a gamble. The front door was to the left but she would have to pass the fireplace. The patio door to the garden was to the right but she would only be able to scream for help and try to heave herself over the fence and into her neighbour's back garden.

Left. She would go left.

There was no time. She had to go.

Just as she was about to throw open the door and run, her phone vibrated in her hand.

If she had more time she probably would have said a small prayer of thanks that she had put it on silent before she got in the shower, but there was no time. She glanced down at the screen as if it might be a miracle. As if it might be the police saying that knew what was happening and they were on their way.

Her breath caught in her throat.

Unknown number.

But the message lit up.

I know you're in there.

Instinct took over and she ran. Not even thinking about her bare feet or the towel that had slipped down over one of her eyes, she gripped the phone in her hand and ran towards the front door. Just before she reached it, she slammed into the man who had stepped into her path. He wrapped his arms around her and her scream was muffled by his torso.

'Hey, hey,' he said.

The man released his grip and took a step backwards.

Relief flooded through her body.

'Oh my god,' she said. 'It's you.'

She thought she was going to burst into tears, but the shock of the last minute had taken hold of her.

'I thought you were skiing,' she said. 'I thought you were away. I just got this text. I was so frightened.'

He let out a low chuckle.

'Sorry to frighten you. I thought I'd be a nice surprise.'

She could only nod and catch her breath.

'But I got this text,' she suddenly stammered. 'And how did you get in here?'

He rubbed her back gently and smiled.

'One thing at a time. What text?'

She turned her screen to show him and he frowned, taking the phone out of her hand to look at it.

'Do you know this number?'

She shook her head.

'Probably someone just joking around with you. I bet it's someone at work who knew you were going to have a quiet night in on your own tonight. Why don't you go and put on some clothes. You must be freezing.'

She took another deep breath and went to head back towards her bedroom. But something didn't feel right.

'The front door was locked. How did you let yourself in?'

He smiled at her and flicked his hair out of his face.

'Your patio door was unlocked. I hopped over from your

neighbour's side. You should really keep that locked. I could have been your anonymous stalker.'

She checked the patio door lock before her shower, didn't she?

Everything suddenly felt like a slightly altered reality. She was second guessing herself, the adrenaline still pumping through her body made her feel jittery and off-balance. She was cold.

'Sweetheart, come here. You're shaking,' he said, his arms outstretched.

She moved towards him and leaned into his body.

'I'm so sorry I scared you. I knocked on the front door but there was no answer. I thought that maybe you had your headphones on so I came around the back and saw your food out on the counter. I tried the door and it was open. When I came in and heard the shower running, I thought I'd get the fire going and surprise you. I hope I'm still a nice surprise?'

She breathed in the scent of him. It was fresh with a hint of something musky, like bergamot. It was an intoxicating scent and she felt like the half glass of wine had gone to her head.

'I'll go and get changed.'

As she moved towards the back of the flat, she could see her keys where she had left them on the kitchen counter. She stopped short as she realized what was missing.

The patio door key. It wasn't on her keychain.

She did not have time to consider how many days ago he had taken it and why she hadn't noticed before now. She did not think about how no one knew she was dating him. She did not think about why this was happening to her. She did not have time to think about anything at all.

Her instinct was to reach for her phone and she whipped around to face him, just in time to see him slip her phone that he had taken from her just a moment before, calmly into the back pocket of his jeans.

Then she saw what was in his other hand.

A knife.

The scar that ran from his lip up towards the bottom of his nose contracted as his face contorted into something she had never seen before. His voice was low, almost a whisper.

'How does it feel to know you are about to die?'

One

Luke was having a difficult time believing where he was standing.

The building in front of him was one that he must have walked by a thousand times before. It was nondescript, mundane, the same colour as the pavement. It was next to the much grander town hall, its steps very familiar to Luke. He had stood on them, grinning and elated, on the day that he married his wife.

That had been a glorious day, just before Christmas. Sadie, who loved the holiday season more than should be permitted, had suggested a winter wedding.

'January?' Luke had said. 'That would be a nice way to begin the year.'

'Oh no,' his wife had replied. 'Three days before Christmas. I've checked and there is availability.'

Luke had hesitated for some reason. When he thinks about it now, he has to shake his head to rid himself of the memory. Why hadn't he immediately agreed? Why didn't he make sure that Sadie had everything she could possibly want for this day? He had pointed out that they may not get that many guests if people were going to be away for the holiday. It was a sentiment that had bemused Sadie.

'I'm going to the town hall to marry you. Who cares if no one else is there?'

In the end, about a dozen guests were with them and the day had been pretty much perfect.

As Luke stared at the steps, he could remember what he felt on that day. It was a joy that he thought would stay with him for the rest of his life. If only he had known that just a few years later he would be standing on the street staring at these steps, his wife was dead and he was about to walk into the building next door to do something he never in his life imagined he would be doing.

Grief counselling.

He was going to group grief counselling.

'I'm sorry you want me to go to what?' he had asked his therapist the week before.

Nicky Bowman had smiled at him and her body betrayed the small chuckle she was having at his expense. As usual, she didn't reply to him straight away, allowing a measure of time to pass for him to connect the dots. But he wasn't connecting anything here.

'I have you,' Luke said. 'I'm not sure that I need to go to further counselling.'

'Well,' Nicky finally replied, 'this is a bit different. I think you might find it very helpful, and very empowering, to experience collective grief.'

'Empowering?'

Luke groaned inside. This was the kind of language that was used at the Met in any kind of "workplace enhancement seminar" about their procedures and well-being. He and Hana despised these seminars.

'What's happening right now?' Nicky asked.

Luke sat up straight, wondering how the hell his therapist

knew what his internal dialogue might have been right there. If he was the kind of person who believed in psychics, he would have wondered if Nicky was one. Instead, he was the kind of person who hated words like "empowering" and would really just like to get on with it.

'Nothing,' he muttered. 'Sorry. Go on.'

As Nicky began to explain her reasonings behind the suggestion of group grief counselling, he had to admit that she may be right.

It had all stemmed from what he had revealed to her just a couple of weeks ago, as the Serious Crime Unit was hunting the gunman who the media eventually named "The London Sniper". As Luke had sat in this office, upstairs in Nicky's house, he had finally told her the truth about his wife's death.

Sadie had been murdered. Her car had not veered off the road into that lake by accident. She had been purposely held under the water and the scene had been staged to cover it up. And Luke and Hana had no idea who had killed her.

The details of why Luke and Hana felt they could not go public with this knowledge were probably equally as shocking to Nicky. She had looked completely stunned as Luke had calmly explained.

'So you think there is someone inside the Metropolitan Police Force who is involved?'

'Or at least protecting someone,' Luke said.

And this is why a couple of weeks later, his therapist was suggesting that he go and grieve alongside some other sad people.

'I think that description is probably a little unfair,' Nicky said. 'Just think about it for a minute. A lot of the space of these sessions we have together is no longer about your grief and your loss. It has inevitably become about your anger and the questions surrounding why this happened to Sadie. And why this happened to you.'

Luke could see that she had a point.

'And if you have another space to talk about what you're feeling in terms of your loss, I'm going to argue that it will only make you more clearheaded going forward when you are trying to figure this out.'

Luke sighed. It was an audible sigh.

'What?' Nicky asked.

'That's exactly what Hana would say.'

———

Luke checked his watch and he couldn't stall any longer. The group grief counselling session was about to start so he finally walked around to the side of the building, as Nicky had instructed, and opened the large glass door.

He could hear voices faintly chattering at the end of the hallway and he was conscious of the sound of his shoes clacking across the hardwood floor that had clearly seen better days. When he reached the end of the hallway, the door into a large, cavernous room was opened. There were a dozen chairs arranged in a circle, most of them occupied, and a man in his forties was standing by a table just to the left of the door, pouring milk into a paper cup of tea.

He looked up at Luke and nodded.

'Am I in the right place for the grief group?' Luke asked, the words suddenly catching in his throat and he hoped that no one had noticed.

'You must be Luke,' the man said. 'Welcome. Would you like a tea or coffee? I'd recommend the tea, myself. This instant stuff is dreadful.'

If he was trying to calm Luke's nerves, the guy was doing a pretty good job.

'Sure,' Luke said. 'A tea would be great. No milk. I guess you know Nicky?'

'Yes,' he replied. 'She's a colleague. I understand that your wife died about eighteen months ago?'

Luke nodded and the man seemed to know to look at him at that exact moment to catch Luke's response, understanding that there would be no verbal answer.

'My name is Michael. You're very welcome to be here and I hope that you'll find it helpful. Most of this group will have suffered a more recent loss than yours, but I imagine that your perspective will be so useful to everyone here. And that theirs will be for you in return.'

Luke accepted the paper cup of tea, needing to hold it by the very top rim as it was scalding hot.

'Come on over,' Michael said. 'I'll introduce you.'

Luke felt like the new kid at school, trying to figure out which chair to approach, scanning the room for the friendliest face. He sat down opposite a pretty young woman, maybe about thirty five years old, who looked at him and nodded a silent hello, her lips pursed together in a slightly defeated smile. Luke was pretty sure that this was the expression often plastered across his own face.

'We have someone new joining us today,' Michael said to the group. 'Luke, would you like to introduce yourself and tell us a little bit about your wife?'

Luke cleared his throat, took a deep breath, and began.

Two

DS Hana Sawatsky could feel the vibration from the treadmill ricocheting up her legs with every step she took. She was just warming up, already slamming her trainers hard onto the machine, trying to shake off the anxiety that had settled into her body since the end of the last case.

It wasn't working particularly well.

Sometimes she felt like she wanted time to slow down, or simply stop so that she could catch her breath. She had too many things to process, too many things to figure out. She envied how her detective partner had somewhere he went every week and dumped everything that was going on in his head onto his therapist. The therapist that she had found for him, no less. But somehow she felt resistant to this for herself. She wondered if releasing the floodgates would result in completely falling apart. That couldn't happen. She often felt like she was the one holding both Luke and herself together. They had a huge responsibility on their shoulders.

They had to figure out who had killed Sadie.

This was as far as she would let her thoughts wander

because if she went any further than this in her mind, she began to spiral into a web of doubt.

And then what?

It wouldn't bring her back. It wouldn't bring back the lives that Luke and Hana and Sadie had lived before. They had to find a way to move on into a different way of living and a new life.

Moving on. Hana used to be very good at doing this, but now she began to wonder if this was true.

The gym that she frequented was closer to her office than her home, which probably said a lot. She spent more time at work than she did relaxing and had noticed of late that even her cat, Max, seemed annoyed when she spent too long at her little mews house in Shoreditch. He clearly felt like it was his house now.

Hana looked around the gym and she didn't recognize any of the usual fitness fanatics that she usually saw on the elliptical machines across from her. She was racking up her miles on the treadmill at a time of day she didn't normally come to the gym. It was only five o'clock in the afternoon and she was usually still at the Met or dealing with something else work related. She took a mental note of the time and thought that she would probably avoid coming back at this time again. While most people would have relished a quieter time in the gym, with people still at work and parents dealing with school pickup time and supper preparation, Hana preferred the gym when it was busy. She could go for a long run on her own outside and clear her head that way but for Hana, the point of a gym was to get lost in a moving, sweating crowd. The noise of the machines, the movement of dozens of bodies, the heat that rose in the room — it all calmed her.

'I struggle to think of anything more abhorrent,' Luke had said to her once as she tried to describe the allure of a gym teeming with testosterone and sweat and pain.

She smiled to herself thinking about Luke's comment, wiping away the first beads of sweat that had begun to form on her forehead. She could never picture him somewhere like this. He didn't understand how it thrilled her, how it relaxed her, and how it reminded her of her old job. The one that she had to run from and yet missed everyday.

You can never escape your past.

And it was her past that kept appearing out of nowhere to remind her of who she was and what she once wanted and the things that had been taken away from her. The thing she had lost.

There had been too much loss.

Hana looked down at the fitness tracker she was wearing on her wrist, feeling annoyed that she was slightly out of breath when she had only been running for five minutes. Her heart rate was higher than it should be at this point in her run and she picked up the pace, stomping her feet harder than was necessary into the rubber track of the treadmill, suddenly furious that her fitness wasn't up to scratch.

At least Hana felt she had enough self-awareness to understand what had recently tipped her over the edge into her present anxiety. As if it wasn't enough that the Serious Crime Unit had been hunting a taunting, sadistic sniper — all of them on edge, waiting for the next shooting to occur and not knowing where he would strike or who he would kill — then Luke had discovered what Sadie had been up to in the months before she died.

She had been at home, for once, when Luke had called. Max had been asleep next to her and Hana had just emerged from a hot shower, trying to rinse away the stress of the past week when she had been racing around the city of London chasing a suspect they couldn't even name until the moments just before they caught him. She had been allowing herself to sink into her exhaustion with a sloppily made gin and tonic and her laptop was open to stream a television series that she had started and forced to abandon due to her job about half a dozen times over the past couple of months.

And then her mobile rang.

She knew immediately that something was wrong when she saw Luke's name on the screen. He had texted her just a couple of hours earlier to let her know that he had decided to take the following day off. Who could blame him? She responded with a thumbs up emoji and contemplated doing the same. So when his name flashed up on her mobile, she knew he wasn't calling to chat.

She didn't even say hello when she picked up. She asked him what was wrong.

'I've found something,' Luke said. 'I don't know what to do with it. I don't really understand it.'

Hana was drawing a blank, having absolutely no idea what he was talking about. For once, she didn't assume that he was talking about Sadie. Except he was.

'What are you talking about, Luke?'

'Sadie's laptop. I logged into it.'

Hana paused before answering, thinking about what they had looked at on her laptop before — just after she died for banking passwords and to cancel subscriptions, and then again when they discovered the truth about her death.

'We did that already. What do you mean?'

'We didn't go through the browsing history, Hana. I had never wanted to look at it before. It was too much. But I've just done it and there was a website that she was constantly on, but it wasn't bookmarked on the laptop, so we didn't catch it before.'

Hana didn't know what to make of this comment. A website wasn't what she thought Luke was going to reveal when he called her.

'What's the website?' she asked, pausing the show she was watching and bringing up the browser on her laptop.

'It's Armchair Investigation Dot Com,' Luke replied.

Hana typed in the url and pressed the return button. It wasn't a particularly slick website and Hana squinted at the screen. The page was a series of posts about crimes — almost all of them were in the UK, and most of them unsolved. Hana recognized many of them but as she clicked into a couple of the posts she could see that they occurred in other jurisdictions of the country and weren't the kind of crimes that would have passed through the Met.

'Okay,' Hana said, 'I'm not really following.'

'The chat forum. At the top of the page. Have you clicked through there yet?'

Hana found the button that Luke was referring to and clicked it. The page opened to a long series of posts in a typical online chat forum, all discussing various crimes.

'Sadie was active in here? She was posting?'

'You're not seeing what I'm seeing, Hana. When I clicked through to the forum, she was still logged into it. I can see what she was posting.'

Hana slowly closed the laptop and slid it off her lap, next to her on the sofa.

'And?'

'And I think you need to come over here.'

———

Now just a few weeks later, Hana and Luke had a better idea of what they were dealing with. Their initial instinct that there was police involvement in Sadie's death may have been right. But what they had uncovered in the armchair investigation forum was something entirely different.

Hana jammed her finger into the incline button on the

treadmill and checked her fitness tracker. She made herself focus on her breathing. Sometimes she found herself holding her breath — for what? With what? Stress, grief, her past suddenly appearing in front of her when she least expected it. All of the above.

She had another half an hour to finish this workout before she needed to have a quick shower and get ready for who she was meeting this evening. Another unexpected person who had called her that morning, another unknown number on her mobile phone. Hana was beginning to wonder when the surprises were going to stop.

Three

Luke wasn't sure what he had been expecting when he sat down in the circle at group grief support. Probably something unbearably sad, and he had been right about that.

It had suddenly struck him when Sadie died that there must be tens of thousands of people walking around the city of London in a state of crushing, crippling grief. These people had been invisible to him before, and indeed were still mostly impossible to spot as they somehow continued on with their normal-looking lives, but he knew that they were carrying around the weight of unbearable loss. Luke found himself sometimes shaking his head as he walked down Upper Street, carrying this same unspeakable weight, ashamed and confounded that he was unaware of this very human experience before now.

He had been so blinkered before. He saw the grief etched on the faces of the families he comforted in his job, those who stood there in shock as he gently but firmly explained that their loved one was dead. And often dead in the most sinister and horrendous of circumstances. Why had he compartmentalized their grief as something unique and terrible, and something that he never thought he would be faced with himself one day?

How ridiculous that he had never considered this for himself.

In this room tonight, every single person's grief was visible to everyone else and that, at least, was a comfort.

When Michael had asked Luke to introduce himself and tell the group a little bit about why he was there, he had been a bit taken aback. He had assumed that as the new person, he would be given the opportunity to listen to everyone else and ease into the slightly overwhelming process of speaking about his grief in front of a group of people.

As he opened his mouth to begin, his brain was flooded with questions. What should he say? What should he not say? What if he said something wrong?

The pretty woman sitting across the circle from him nodded her head and smiled. Her eyes looked tired and Luke imagined that without a sheen of grief, they probably were bright and they probably sparkled. She smiled encouragingly at him.

'My name is Luke,' he began. 'Thanks very much for letting me join you all today. I have to say, I feel a bit nervous and didn't expect that.'

There was a gentle murmur of laughter amongst the group, which broke the ice a little bit.

'I'm here because I lost my wife, Sadie, a little over a year ago. I'm sorry to say, especially if some of you have only recently lost someone, that I just don't feel any better than I did right after she died.'

Luke trailed off after he said this, unsure of what else to offer.

'One of the first things we talk about here,' Michael said, jumping in and for which Luke felt grateful, 'is that grief is grief. No one's emotions are better or worse than anyone else's and we all move through this process at different rates and in our own time. So don't worry about that. Why don't you tell us a little bit about Sadie, so we can all get to know her?'

Luke was unprepared for the relief that flooded through his body as he began to talk about his wife. He hadn't spoken about her — introduced her — to anyone since he began seeing Dr. Nicky Bowman all those months ago. It was wonderful to tell the group about her. How beautiful she was, how successful she had been in her career so she retired in her thirties and spent her time and her money on projects and causes close to her heart.

But then Luke found himself telling this group of strangers about all of his wife's quirkiness.

'She was obsessed with sudoku and I would find puzzles all over the house, ripped out of newspapers and half completed. She insisted that if she squinted her eyes at the difficult ones that the numbers would suddenly jump out and make sense to her. And I swear to god they did. It was bizarre. She used to walk around the house when she brushed her teeth. I would find her toothbrush next to the kitchen sink one day and the downstairs bathroom sink the next, and one time I found it outside by the garden hosepipe. She was forever asking me where her toothbrush was in the morning and just before bed. I miss that.'

The entire room was smiling at him and Luke smiled back. He shifted in his chair and looked towards Michael, signalling that while he could talk about Sadie for the rest of the evening, he was aware that he had probably said enough and it was time for someone else to have a turn addressing the group.

As Luke listened to these strangers — some spoke about their deceased loved one and others spoke about their own day to day existence that was now a shock to the system without them — he found that he recognized at least one element of every single person's story. He knew instantly why Nicky had urged him to come here. He felt less alone.

The hour had come to a close and Michael confirmed that the group would meet at the same place and same time the following week. As they were stacking the chairs back against the wall, Michael approached Luke.

'I hope you'll be back again next week? You would be so welcome.'

Luke smiled at him.

'You bet. Unless something comes up at work, I'll be here. Thanks for including me.'

Luke shrugged into his jacket and walked over to the tea and coffee table where a few people were still chatting. He felt he needed to say goodbye properly as it would be rude to rush off after being witness to so many deeply personal stories.

As he thanked everyone for welcoming him so warmly and then turned to leave, the pretty woman from across the circle placed her hand on his arm. Luke was startled slightly, and looked down at her hand on his arm. Her wedding ring looked shiny against her pale skin. The woman had lost her husband only a few weeks earlier. He wondered how long they had been married. The woman leaned into Luke and whispered.

'Can I talk to you for a minute?'

She gestured that they should move away from the group, although Luke wasn't sure that anyone was paying particular attention to them.

'Sure.'

As they stepped aside, Luke struggled to remember her name. Everything had been a bit of a blur over the last hour.

She stopped just a few feet away from the others and placed her hands on each hip, as if she was preparing to perform a yoga move.

'Evie,' she said, as if on cue.

'Right. Evie. Yes.'

She smiled at Luke again, as she had been throughout the entire session.

'Look, I wonder if you'd like to get a cup of coffee?'

The last thing Luke had expected walking into this room in this building next to where he got married was this. He was completely taken aback and opened his mouth to respond, but no sound came out.

'Sorry,' Evie said, noticing his discomfort. 'I don't mean to be forward, it's just that we are around the same age and have both lost our spouses and I just thought we might have more to talk about.'

Luke felt sympathy for her, but simultaneously felt uncomfortable. It had been quite enough to come to this grief support group in the first place and continuing to chat over a coffee with a woman he didn't know seemed like a step too far somehow.

He was also acutely aware that this woman was attractive and looking at him in a way that he knew meant she was interested in him.

Luke couldn't believe it when he found himself saying yes to her offer and following her out the door.

Four

Luke stirred his cortado, dismayed to see how milky it seemed to be. He was paying particular attention to it because he found himself feeling slightly nervous every time he looked directly at Evie, who was sitting across from him.

He took a sip and took a moment to swallow it before gently placing the cup back down onto the table and taking a breath.

'Thanks so much for taking the time,' Evie said.

'Oh sure.'

Evie looked equally nervous, which was a small comfort. She seemed smaller in person now that he was up close to her, not across the room in a circle of people. He noticed that she had gentle highlights in her hair that you could only see when she brushed it away from her face. This made Luke think of his wife. He could almost hear Sadie whisper in his ear, 'Those are expensive.' She was always so aware of the specific grooming practices of other people — and what they must have cost.

Luke suddenly felt guilty sitting in this cafe with another woman. It must have looked like they were on a date.

'It's a lovely cafe,' Evie ventured, trying to instigate some sort of conversation that didn't revolve around their dead spouses.

Luke turned and looked at the room. Evie was right — it was a small, but beautifully decorated cafe with glass candle holders and little vases of flowers on each table. The lighting was cozy and the tables, crucially, weren't too close together. The ambiance made up for the lacklustre espresso.

'Yes,' Luke replied. 'Do you usually come here after the group session?'

'Oh no, I've never been in here before. Always thought about it, though. Usually I find the group counselling quite exhausting and I tend to just head straight home.'

Luke nodded, feeling a little exhausted himself.

'How did you come across the group?' Luke asked.

'My therapist,' Evie replied.

Luke couldn't help but laugh.

'Me too. Thank god for our therapists.'

Evie also laughed and it felt like the tension in the air between them melted away instantly. The ice had been broken.

'To be honest,' Luke continued. 'I never thought I'd be the kind of person who would see a therapist. It wasn't anything I had ever considered before this.'

This.

Even with two people recently bereaved, it was sometimes just too difficult to say "when my wife died".

Evie ran her fingers through her hair again and then around the rim of her coffee cup.

'I know it's rather speaking the obvious, but I'm so sorry for the loss of your wife,' she said.

'Thanks. And same to you. I'm very sorry.'

'You said her name was Sadie, is that right?'

Luke nodded.

'I loved hearing about her tonight,' Evie said. ' I think everyone did. It's so hard to get your head around the fact that they won't be introduced to anyone new ever again. Or at least that's what I can't help but think about whenever I talk about Johnny to the group.'

A lump began to form in Luke's throat. Could it be that he had never entertained this thought before? He hadn't realized that no one would ever be introduced to his wife for the first time again. Luke thought constantly about all of the people who knew Sadie and mourned her deeply, but somehow it hadn't occurred to him that anyone new in his life would never meet her in the first place.

Luke tried to shake this thought away, or at least push it aside to deal with later — such a common trick with the mind games one plays with grief.

'You've only just recently lost him?' Luke said, not able to remember exactly what Evie had said that evening in the group.

'It's coming up to a month now. I can hardly believe it. It still doesn't feel real.'

'I'm so sorry. It's probably not helpful to say that it still doesn't feel real to me either. And for me it has been almost eighteen months.'

'Shit,' said Evie, in the most matter-of-fact way.

Luke couldn't help but laugh. For a split second, something about her response reminded Luke of his wife.

As they kept chatting, the conversation veered away from the painful details of their respective losses and towards the sometimes cringe-worthy reactions of acquaintances who didn't know how to speak to them after Sadie and Johnny had died. Luke and Evie found themselves giggling and ordering another cup of coffee, as their chat moved along further to discuss aspects of their everyday lives. It suddenly felt like a very normal conversation between a man and a woman who were getting to know each other. The preceding hour and a half almost vanished from memory and Luke felt himself relaxing.

He couldn't believe it, but he was all of a sudden having a nice time. Thoughts of what was to come next were pushed out of his mind. The itch of wondering if he was actually on a date refused to be scratched. He could not go there. He just wanted to enjoy the moment.

'Do you live around here?' Luke asked.

'Not too far. I'm just down City Road, closer to Old Street tube station.'

Luke noticed that Evie's demeanour suddenly shifted — her body tensed up and she opened her mouth to speak again, but it took her a moment to find the words.

'I've only been back there for a few days,' she said. 'I couldn't be there after Johnny died. I've been staying with my sister.'

Luke knew this feeling. He had stayed on the sofa in Hana's living room for a couple of nights after Sadie died. It was torturous to be alone.

As he expressed this thought to Evie, she immediately shook her head and Luke stopped talking.

'No...it's just that...well, you weren't at the first couple of sessions where the grief support group met, so you don't know. Johnny went over the balcony of our flat. We live on the fourteenth floor.'

A wave of sympathy rushed over Luke as Evie explained. To lose your partner so early in life was difficult enough, but to lose them by suicide must be exquisitely painful.

'I'm so sorry,' Luke said.

Evie clearly wanted to change the subject and asked Luke about how he met Sadie.

'Oh in the very usual, very boring way. I was at a pub with

friends and someone knew one of her friends that was there and we all got chatting and that was that. She asked me out, actually. It was a very Sadie thing to do. I'm rather hopeless at these kinds of things.'

'I doubt that very much,' Evie replied.

'What about you?' Luke asked. 'How did you meet Johnny.'

Evie hesitated again before answering.

'I don't really remember. Would you excuse me for a second?'

Luke smiled at her, feeling like he had somehow put his foot in it.

'Oh sure, of course.'

Evie thanked him and stood up, placing her hand on Luke's shoulder for a brief moment before walking towards the loos at the back of the cafe.

As Luke waited for her to return, he wondered if he was going to tell Hana about this part of his evening. He pulled his phone out of his pocket to check the time and was relieved that there were no missed calls or texts from Hana. They had spoken about maybe having a drink and going through some of the forum posts on the website where Sadie had been lurking before her death after their respective plans that evening. But now Luke really didn't feel up to it.

Evie returned and slid back into the chair across from Luke. There was an awkward pause now that their conversation had been interrupted and its natural flow was gone. It was Evie who spoke first.

'Luke, I need to tell you something.'

Luke felt suddenly uneasy, as if he was caught somewhere he shouldn't be.

'Okay,' was all he could say, in a tone that he hoped sounded natural.

'I knew who you were the moment you stepped through

the door tonight. I hope that doesn't sound strange. But with the London Sniper case a few weeks ago, you were all over the news.'

'Right,' Luke said, feeling relieved. He often forgot that he wasn't completely anonymous thanks to his job, although the last case would have made him more publicly visible than he would have been in years.

'And I knew that I needed to speak to you privately after the group. It seemed like this was something sent from heaven for me. A sign.'

'I'm not exactly following,' Luke said, chuckling softly. 'How am I a sign?'

'Because you are a detective. A senior detective.'

Luke didn't say anything, but stared at this pretty woman's face. Her eyes suddenly looked desperate.

'My husband,' Evie said. 'I think he was murdered.'

Five

The phone call for Hana had come out of the blue and Laura Rowdy had been standing in front of Hana when it had come in. It was clear from the look on Rowdy's face as Hana spoke to the voice on the other end of the line that Rowdy knew exactly who was calling.

Hana had actually closed her eyes in exasperation, understanding instantly who had given the caller her phone number.

You could never stay angry at Rowdy for long.

Laura Rowdy was a bit of a legend at the Met and both Hana and Luke wondered if everything would fall apart there if she was ever to leave. Hana actually wasn't entirely sure what her exact job title was — it didn't really matter. She was as integral to the Serious Crime Unit as Santa Claus was to Christmas. If you needed something that seemed impossible to get, if you weren't sure how two things connected but knew that it was crucial to find out and even more crucial to have it done as quickly as possible, Rowdy was always going to come to the rescue.

She was universally adored at the Unit, and begrudgingly respected by even the most irritating colleagues. Although their boss, Chief Superintendent Stephen O'Donell was one of the biggest wastes of space at the Met, he knew not to cross Laura Rowdy.

Hana could see O'Donnell pacing around his office, also on the phone, looking like he was about to throttle someone. She made a mental note to get out of there as soon as she could, not wanting to be the team member called in to deal with something that she clearly did not want to be dealing with.

The voice on the other end of the phone didn't speak for long. She didn't need to. Arrangements were made to meet later that evening and Hana hung up.

'You gave her my mobile number,' Hana said, less an accusation and more of a resignation.

'I did,' Rowdy replied, unapologetically.

Hana didn't know exactly what to say to Rowdy here. She would have trusted her with most information, but this was personal.

'But I want to assure you that I didn't give out your number without being asked for it.'

Hana was slightly incredulous at this comment, but she also knew that Rowdy was right.

'Does Luke know that she wanted to be in touch with me?'

'He does not,' Rowdy replied.

'Okay, thanks.'

Hana looked down the hall at O'Donnell again and decided to pick up her coat and get out of the office for a bit. She would have time to go to the gym before the meeting that was set for seven o'clock that evening.

'Hana,' Rowdy called after her, making Hana stop in her tracks and turn around.

'Yes?'

'It's okay to open up sometimes you know. I worked with her for a long time. You can trust her.'

Hana raised her eyebrows as the lift doors opened.

'Rowdy, I love the sentiment. But I hardly know a single thing about you.'

Laura Rowdy smiled and walked back to her office.

———

Hana had showered quickly after her workout in the gym and made her way to a Turkish restaurant in the centre of town. It was on a bustling pedestrian-only block of shops and restaurants and felt like a strange place to be meeting for a private conversation where you probably didn't wish to be seen.

She opened the door and was surprised to see that the restaurant was half empty. It was dark and the light in the room had a red tinge, created by the red glass jars on each table that were flickering with candlelight. Plush, velvet cushions adorned each chair and the smell of the restaurant was incredible. The spices, mostly cumin and thyme and cinnamon, made Hana's mouth water. She was also starving after her session on the treadmill.

The two waiters were standing at the back of the restaurant, near to the door to the kitchen. They looked up when Hana entered and then continued with their tasks, not moving forward to attend to her.

Great service, Hana thought. Then she saw why they didn't move. Philippa Nicolson was sitting at a table at the very back of the restaurant and she was clearly waiting for someone.

She was waiting for DS Hana Sawatsky.

Hana walked to the table and stood in front of it, shrugging off her coat and draping it over the empty chair across from Philippa. She waited to be invited to sit down, an automatic habit for someone much senior than her rank. Even though Philippa Nicolson was retired, Hana was slightly nervous of her.

'Sawatsky,' Philippa said. 'Good evening. Please.' She gestured towards the empty chair.

'Ma'am,' Hana said, easing herself into the seat and pressing her lower back into the velvet cushion to give herself a little more room.

'Hungry? The food here is incredible. I've been coming here for years.'

Hana looked around for a menu, but didn't see one. Philippa gestured to one of the waiters, who again did not approach the table, but hurried back inside the kitchen. He emerged a moment later with two plates of steaming falafel and dumpling and placed them in front of Philippa and Hana.

'What would you like to drink?' Philippa asked.

Realizing that she was probably in for more than she bargained for, Hana looked at the waiter and sighed.

'I think I'm going to need a gin and tonic.'

The waiter nodded and Philippa picked up her large glass of red wine and took a sip.

'I've never come across this restaurant before,' Hana said, suddenly wondering what the hell she was doing here.

'Isn't it perfect?'

Hana knew what Philippa meant. If you wanted a quiet meal and you wanted it to be private, but you needed to stay in the centre of London, this was a very good bet.

'Turkish food is great. Thank you.'

'Do you smoke, Sawatsky?'

'Uh, no.'

'Not even one cheeky cigarette after a few G&Ts?'

'Afraid not, Ma'am. I've never smoked.'

'Well,' Philippa said, 'good for you. I, on the other hand, am partial to a cigarette even though I quit many years ago.

Allegedly. And when you're the last table here, the waiters lock the door and bring you an ashtray. I discovered that about fifteen years ago and have been coming here ever since.'

Hana had no response to this, thinking about the five miles she had just run on the treadmill. She reached forward and helped herself to a dumpling. She was starving and felt like she needed her wits about her for this conversation. A gin and tonic on an empty stomach was a bad idea.

'And?' Philippa asked, pointing to the plates of food.

'Excellent,' Hana replied, her mouth still full.

Philippa sipped her wine again and leaned back in her chair against the velvet cushions.

'I suppose you're wondering why I asked you to dinner.'

Hana wiped her mouth and happily accepted the drink that the waiter had brought over to the table.

'I am, yes.'

'You did excellent work on the Grace Feist case last year. It was a hell of a few days.'

'It was,' Hana said. 'It was very good of you to come back to help us. But, of course, it must also have been difficult for you.'

Hana's comment was only a massive understatement.

The girl that had been fished out of the canal in East London was not the same girl as on the identification they had found with her. She was Grace Feist, who had been kidnapped as a child almost seven years earlier and never been found. Until they found her and realized that she had been kept prisoner this entire time.

Philippa Nicolson had worked the initial Grace Feist case with Luke all of those years ago and although she had retired only a year after Grace had gone missing, Philippa had come back to help them find who had kidnapped her and then killed her almost seven years later.

Hana was no less intimidated by Philippa sitting in the

Turkish restaurant than she had been a few months earlier during that case.

'The drink we had at the pub while we were hunting Grace's killer was interrupted,' Philippa said.

'Yes.'

'We were just getting to know each other.'

Hana raised her eyebrows.

'Is that what that drink was about? I thought you were interviewing me, making sure I was up to scratch to be Luke's partner after you.'

'Well, it was a little bit of that, too,' Philippa said, helping herself to some falafel.

'Are you continuing the interview all of these months later? That seems unlikely. I'm just not that interesting. And Luke is fine.'

'That was going to be my next question.'

Hana didn't bite at this comment. She took a sip of her drink and made a concerted effort to not cross her arms. She didn't want to look defensive in any way. She liked Philippa Nicolson, but she also didn't understand why the hell she was here and what she wanted.

'How are both of you doing?' Philippa asked. 'It still must be very hard to cope with the loss of Sadie.'

'I don't imagine that it will ever be easy,' Hana replied. 'But I suppose we are built to withstand grief. Human beings are very resilient.'

'Are they? I guess so. You certainly seem to be.'

What the hell did that mean, Hana thought, suddenly feeling like the tables were being turned on her and she didn't know why.

'I was concerned for you after the Grace Feist case,' Philippa said. 'With what happened.'

Hana should have felt her body relax at this point. If this was why Philippa had asked to meet with her, it was an extremely nice gesture. Hana had been kidnapped herself, drugged, and held for several hours before she was rescued. She tried not to think about it — what good would that do? But it took a bit of effort to keep it pushed out of her mind.

'Thank you,' Hana said, softly.

'Look, Hana. You're wondering why on earth I've asked you to meet me. Partly I wanted to see you again properly after the Grace Feist case. We were all thrown in the deep end together and you went through something very difficult. I'm glad to see that you've been able to move on. I know that can't be easy.'

Hana waited for her to continue.

'And if you remember, when we went for that drink, I had asked you why you left the forces and joined the Metropolitan Police.'

Hana did not need to be reminded of this. At the time, she had frozen in place when Philippa had asked her this question. She had frozen in place because of what Philippa had said next. She had casually mentioned that she had asked Rowdy to pull her personnel file, which Rowdy had done. At the time Philippa said that she was simply trying to get to know the new detective that had taken her place and was now working with DCI Luke Wiley. But some of the file was blank. It had been redacted. And what was missing was the reason and the circumstances surrounding her abrupt move from her old job to her new one at the Met.

'The thing is,' Philippa said, 'that missing part of the file... the one that was above my rank and had been sealed. I managed to get my hands on it.'

Six

As Luke pulled his phone out of his pocket after saying goodbye to Evie outside the cafe, he took a moment to decide who to call. Watching her walk down the street towards City Road, he wondered how his evening had turned into something this bizarre. Part of him wanted to call Nicky to tell her that he wouldn't be attending the group grief support again. But instead he called Hana because he could really use a drink. That cortado didn't even come close.

The call went straight to voicemail as if Hana had cancelled it, but a text flashed up on his screen a couple of seconds later that said she would ring him in a minute.

Upper Street was surprisingly busy for a weekday evening and Luke weaved around people out for dinner or watching the football at the pubs and cocktail bars that dotted the strip of activity that ran about a half a mile long. He needed to walk and clear his head after such a bizarre conversation with Evie, but he also didn't want to head home alone where he knew he would inevitably keep thinking about it.

When Hana rang back, he suggested that they meet for a drink and she eagerly accepted. She said she had been at a quick dinner but had just finished and would meet him for a mid-evening nightcap at the wine bar that was on her way home and only a little out of Luke's way.

When Luke arrived at the wine bar he chuckled to himself as he always did when he looked at the sign out front. The bar was called Enoki, after the particular species of mushroom, and the logo plastered on the sign and the menu made Hana grimace. She despised mushrooms, which is why they only drank at this wine bar, and never ordered the small plates of food.

Hana was already sitting up at the bar, a large glass of red in front of her. Luke pulled out the chair next to her and sat down.

'I hear the mushroom focaccia is great here. Shall we?'

Hana slowly turned her head to look at him and no retort was offered. Luke realized that she didn't seem to be in the mood his poor attempt at humour.

'Where were you tonight?' he asked. 'I expected you to be at home when I rang and I was going to have to invite myself over there.'

Hana swirled her wine glass, the liquid almost jumping past the rim, but not quite.

'It was a bit of a weird one tonight,' Hana replied.

'I'm pretty sure I'm going to be able to top it, but go ahead.'

Hana took a sip of her wine while Luke gestured to the bartender that he would have the same.

'I was having dinner with Philippa Nicolson,' Hana said.

Luke looked genuinely taken aback, not a facial expression that Hana was used to seeing. He was usually so good to take in information without any hint of what he was thinking, digest it internally, and then respond.

'Philippa? What was she doing in London? Why? Why didn't you tell me?'

Hana knew that these questions would be peppered at her and she wished that she had expanded on the situation, instead of dropping an unexpected piece of information without context. But she also had thought through exactly what she was going to say to Luke about the dinner — and what she was not going to say.

'I think she was speaking to Rowdy about something and then asked if I was around. I was, and Philippa was in town for something else, and asked if I wanted to grab a bite to eat. I think she just wanted to check in with me after what happened. It was nice of her.'

Hana knew that Luke would feel slighted that his old partner on the force had reached out to Hana — his current partner — for dinner, instead of reaching out to Luke. But Hana also knew that if she played the 'I was kidnapped and held by a sadistic and twisted killer' card, that she could get away with it. Luke still felt a bit guilty for letting Hana be put in that situation, and she knew that if she mentioned it, that not much more would be said.

Hana was right.

Luke murmured that it was, indeed, a lovely gesture and then he gratefully accepted his own glass of wine from the bartender.

'Well, you're not going to believe my night,' he said.

'Try me.'

'I went to a grief counselling support group. Nicky recommended it.'

Hana burst out laughing.

'You. In a group of people. Talking about your feelings.'

'That's not even the half of it.'

'Okay,' said Hana, suddenly feeling the tension in her body begin to release. 'What happened?'

'I think,' Luke said afterwards. 'That I then ended up on a small date.'

It took Hana a moment to collect herself and make sure she heard him correctly.

'What the hell is a *small date*?'

'Well,' said Luke, who had also decided to lie by omission to his partner, 'there was this very nice woman there who had also lost her spouse. As we were putting things away after the group session, she came up to me and asked if I wanted to grab a coffee.'

'And you said yes?' Hana said incredulously.

'It was all incredibly awkward. It just sort of happened.'

'It just sort of *happened*?'

'Hana,' Luke said, trying to stop any further questions. He could feel the heat beginning to rise in his neck.

'Sorry,' Hana said. 'Tell me about it.'

'Honestly, it was nothing except a sort of bizarre coffee. I kept wondering what the hell I was doing there.'

'What does she look like?'

'Are you actually serious?'

'What?' Hana said, completely unapologetically.

'Not exactly a question that's in solidarity of feminism.'

'Oh spare me. What does she look like?'

Luke sighed.

'She's maybe a little younger than me. Early thirties? Cute. I don't know. It wasn't really the point.'

Hana lowered her voice to a husky whisper.

'It wasn't really the point?'

'Jesus, Hana.'

'Well, did it feel like she was asking you out?'

Luke hesitated for just a moment and he hoped that Hana did not notice.

'No. It didn't feel like that. I think she was just lonely and traumatized after losing her husband. I rather know the feeling.'

At this last comment, Hana reached over and squeezed

Luke's arm. She wanted to ask the question that she knew she shouldn't ask and so didn't.

Did Luke think that he would ever date again?

Luke had known Hana for a long time, and so he knew that she was thinking this quietly to herself. He was relieved that she did not voice the question aloud.

It was clear that they had both had quite enough of speaking about the circumstances of their particular evenings, and so they continued into their own evening and thought that they may as well get a bottle. It was very good wine.

Seven

Hangovers from red wine have a particular edge to them and Luke actually had difficulty peeling his tongue from the roof of his mouth when he woke up. He wanted to stretch out in his comfortable bamboo sheets, but knew that any movement of his head before he had a chance to take some painkillers was going to hurt.

Sure enough, as he propped himself up on one elbow and reached over to the drawer in his bedside table, it felt like his brain was rattling around in his skull and there was no cushioning in there. He got a couple of pills into his mouth and gulped down some water from a pint glass he had somehow miraculously thought to bring to bed with him when he had returned home from Enoki. Hana and Luke had stayed there until closing and that bottle was followed by another one.

By the time he finally arrived at New Scotland Yard, having been revived by a steaming shower and two cups of wickedly strong coffee — Guatemalan beans freshly ground — he was beginning to feel a bit more human.

Then he saw Hana, her short hair pulled back by an elastic band that was somehow staying in place and a small smear of yesterday's mascara lingering under her right eye. The size of the egg and bacon sandwich that she was holding, half of it already consumed, had to be seen to be believed. Next to that was a can of Coke Zero. The smell was absolutely nauseating.

Luke grimaced and didn't say anything to her, instead walking past Hana and into his office where he gently shut the door behind him. He had barely had time to take off his jacket and press the button on his computer monitor before there was a knock at the door.

It was a little louder than was strictly necessary.

He knew it had to be Rowdy.

'Yeah,' he said towards the direction of the door.

Rowdy's head popped inside and she was smirking.

'At least you look a little better than Sawatsky. Fun night?'

'I'm fine, Rowdy. What's up?'

'Well, at least it's a quiet day. You asked for the forensic files on the Waller case to be brought up for cross referencing. They've arrived. Do you want me to sort them first? I have the time.'

Just as Luke opened his mouth to reply, the sound of multiple phones ringing through the Serious Crime Unit broke the quiet hum of the floor. Luke and Rowdy stared at each other for a brief second and then Rowdy disappeared back into the unit. There was no point in Luke answering his mobile which was buzzing in the inside pocket of his jacket that he had only just draped across the back of his office chair. He knew that Rowdy would be telling him where he had to go.

Luke stood back up, his head still feeling fragile, and he pulled his jacket off the chair and headed back into the hallway. As he shrugged it on, Hana was downing the last dregs of her Coke Zero and balling up the wrapper from her sandwich.

They both looked over at Rowdy who was listening

intently to whoever was on the phone. She hung up and turned to the detectives.

'So much for your quiet day. The body of a woman has been found in her home. Officers responded to a call from her cleaning lady. I'll text you the address.'

'You're driving,' Hana said to Luke. 'My head is absolutely splitting.'

———

The Venetian Tower was thirty two floors high. A residential building like this was unusual for London, something that would be more at home in Chicago or Miami. Architecturally, it was interesting but not offensive with just enough glass to make it shimmer but not too many angles to make it ugly next to its neighbouring buildings.

Hana leaned forward in the passenger seat as they were parking outside on a side street that ran off the main road, craning her neck to look up at it.

'I think there is a pool on the roof,' she said.

'No,' replied Luke. 'That the one south of the river. But I'm sure there is a pool in here somewhere. And a cinema and gym, I bet.'

'Would you live somewhere like this?'

Luke knew that it was a rhetorical question, as this building was the exact opposite of the house he lived in that his wife had designed.

'Let's head inside,' Luke said.

The paramedics who had been sent to the scene from the emergency dispatcher were finishing packing their gear into the back of the ambulance. One of the crew spotted Luke and Hana walking towards the door and called out.

'Detectives.'

Luke and Hana paused and turned to her direction. The woman approached them and was clearly shaken.

'Good morning,' Luke said.

'I'm glad you're here,' the woman said, which seemed like an odd remark.

'Were you able to administer any kind of care?' Hana asked.

The woman shook her head.

'Any attempt at resuscitation when you arrived?'

'There was absolutely nothing we could do,' the woman said. 'It is extremely difficult up there.'

Hana thanked her and they watched the woman walk back towards the ambulance.

'Well that doesn't sound good,' said Hana.

They continued on into the lobby of the building and several police officers were now in place, taking names of anyone entering or exiting. The older man dressed in a suit was wringing his hands as he spoke to an officer.

Luke flashed his badge and introduced himself. The officer explained that this was the building's overnight concierge who was just finishing his shift when police cars screamed up to the building and demanded to be escorted up to the fourteenth floor.

Hana was asking the concierge a question, but Luke didn't hear it. The nausea that had abated suddenly rose quickly from his stomach into his chest and he had to swallow. He told himself to breathe.

'What floor is the deceased on?' he asked the officer.

'Fourteenth, Sir.'

Luke interrupted Hana and looked directly at the concierge.

'Do you know the woman who has died?' he asked.

'Yes,' the concierge said, his voice shaking. 'It's so awful. She is a very nice lady.'

'Do we have a name?' Luke said, to no one in particular.

The officer looked down at his pad.

'Yes. The deceased is Evelyn Glover.'

Evelyn. Evie.

'It's just terrible,' the concierge said. 'Her husband only just died a few weeks ago.'

'I know,' said Luke.

Hana looked at him, wondering what the hell was going on.

Eight

The detectives were alone in the lift as they rose up from the lobby to the fourteenth floor.

'We need to get Dr. Chung here,' Luke said.

'She will already have been called. What the hell is going on?'

Luke was not aware that he was shaking his head slowly, back and forth, almost like he was in a trance. He licked his lips, trying to quell the nausea that was still lingering and he knew was about to rise up again the moment he walked into the flat.

'It's Evie. From last night. From the group counselling session and the coffee. She said that she lived on the fourteenth floor.'

Hana looked at the buttons above the lift door lighting up as they rose up by each floor and knew that they did not have much time.

'Tell me quickly.'

Luke snapped out of his trance and lowered his voice, speaking as clearly and rapidly as he could. He also knew that when the lift doors opened, they would need to stop communicating about Luke's involvement with Evie the previous evening.

'She said that she had recognized me from the news when we were hunting the London Sniper and that she wanted to speak to me privately. Her husband died by falling from the balcony of this flat, but she said that she was convinced he did not kill himself. She believed that he had been murdered.'

Hana couldn't help herself.

'You could not have told me this last night at Enoki?' she hissed.

Luke ignored her and looked at the buttons. They were at the twelve floor.

'What do you think?' Hana continued. 'Was her husband murdered?'

'I don't know. I didn't get a good sense last night. I was taken aback and just listened to her. I figured that I would deal with it later if I ever saw her again.'

The lift reached the fourteenth floor and Luke knew that he was about to see her again, just not in the way he had expected. There were two police officers speaking to someone a couple of doors down from Evie's flat, which was towards the end of the hallway on the lefthand side. Police tape had already been hastily put up across the door and Luke gently lifted it up so that Hana could duck underneath and then he did the same.

Dr. Chung, the medical examiner that worked for both the coroner and the Metropolitan Police Force, was already inside. She was dressed in a white, sterile jumpsuit and her gloved hands were holding her phone. She had been squinting at the screen and looked up at the detectives as they entered.

'You're going to need at least foot protectors,' Dr. Chung said. 'It's a mess in here.'

Hana and Luke looked at each other. Dr. Chung was a no

nonsense, no hyperbole kind of colleague. This did not bode well.

'I'll fetch them for you, Sir,' said one of the officers stationed by the front door to the flat.

Hana and Luke accepted the plastic foot covers and slipped them over their shoes.

'The body is this way,' said Dr. Chung.

The hallway from the front door towards the rear of the flat was quite narrow and there were two doors leading from it, one on the left and one on the right. The walls were painted a bright white and looked pristine. There was no mess in sight, so the detectives knew that whatever had happened, Evie hadn't made it to the front door. If she had tried to escape, she hadn't made it this far.

As Luke and Hana approached the rear of the flat, the unmistakable metallic smell of blood was noticeable and they knew that only a large amount of blood would result in such an odour. As they walked into the large open plan living room and kitchen, light from the floor to ceiling windows flooded the flat. Luke immediately noticed the balcony doors and thought of Evie's husband going over the side to his death. It was a long way down. There would have been enough time to think about what was happening to you.

'Jesus,' said Hana.

'I know,' replied Dr. Chung.

Evie's body looked small and completely broken. She was lying on the living room sofa, her eyes wide open and her mouth smeared with blood.

Blood was everywhere. Evie was covered in it except for patches of skin on her cheeks and forehand, now with the pale blue tinge of death. Her right arm was at a terrible angle.

'Her shoulder has been badly dislocated,' said Dr. Chung. 'Whoever did this really dragged her around the flat.'

'I hope she was already dead,' said Hana.

'Sadly, DS Sawatsky, I don't believe she was.'

Luke closed his eyes. This could not be happening. He could hear Evie's laugh from last night and thought about the way she fiddled with her coffee cup as she carefully chose the words she wanted to describe her feelings of deep grief. He thought about the way she touched his shoulder when she excused herself momentarily to use the washroom.

Luke tried to think back to the last thing Evie had said to him as they parted ways on Upper Street the previous evening. In actual fact, it had just been over twelve hours earlier. Did she say anything that would have hinted that she was nervous or thought that she may be in danger?

There had been a slightly awkward moment where they did not know what the correct goodbye should be for two people who had been strangers to each other just a couple of hours earlier but had shared some intimate details of their lives and their difficult losses. Luke felt it was too formal to shake her hand and far too intimate to lean down and kiss Evie on the cheek, so he had just stood there like an awkward teenager.

Evie was as warm and generous as she had been all evening and leaned in to give Luke a small hug. As Luke thought about it now and looked at her corpse, his nausea began to swell again. And he felt angry — not only at whatever monster had done this to her, but also angry at himself. Why hadn't he walked her home? It wasn't all that far from where they had enjoyed their cup of coffee. He had been uncomfortable by her revelation about her husband's potential murder and had wanted to get out of there and away from her. It had been a mistake.

'There was nothing you could have done, Luke.'

Hana always could sense what he was thinking. For once Luke knew that his face was betraying his private thoughts.

'And Luke, you have to go now,' Hana said.

He nodded. He knew that he was one of the last people to

see Evie alive and that his own whereabouts would have to be verified. Luke was going to have to have himself cleared by his own unit.

'I'm calling Rowdy and asking her to send Joy Lombardi over. When you get back to the Met, insist that Sharma looks at the CCTV to clear you. Call Enoki and have them verify as well. You need to get this done as quickly as possible.'

Luke looked at Evie one last time.

'I know.'

Nine

The look on Dr. Chung's face when she heard why Luke was suddenly leaving the crime scene was one that simultaneously portrayed shock and a bit of *this would only happen to DCI Wiley*. She would continue the initial examination with Hana and then have the body moved to her lab after the forensics team had finished with what they needed.

As Luke was pulling off his foot protectors and stepping outside the door, he suddenly stopped. He called for Dr. Chung and Hana, who popped their heads around the corner from the living room. When Luke beckoned for them, the two women joined him at the front door.

'Dr. Chung, do you have an approximate time of death yet?'

She nodded and Hana found that she was biting her lower lip in anticipation.

'She is almost in complete rigor mortis, so she died approximately eleven to twelve hours ago.'

Luke closed his eyes with relief. He and Hana were still in Enoki on only on their first bottle of red at that point.

'Thanks. Good luck. Hana, I'll call when I can.'

Hana said nothing but nodded and headed back into the flat. Dr. Chung hung back at the front door.

'Wiley,' she said. 'I'll know more when I get her back to the lab, but whoever did this really wanted to hurt her.'

'Okay,' was all Luke could say, very softly.

As Luke stepped back into the lift, he dialled Rowdy and told her that he was coming back in.

'Is O'Donnell still in? I'm going to need to speak to him.'

'He is. In a foul temper as usual. What's going on?'

'You won't believe it. I'll explain when I get back but in the meantime, I need Sharma over at the unit as quickly as you can get him there.'

'Sharma has been reassigned to Covert Policing for a special Taskforce at the moment. He'll be there another couple of weeks, I imagine.'

Shit, Luke thought.

'Laura, I really need him.'

The use of Rowdy's first name immediately indicated the seriousness with which this situation needed to be dealt with. She could only recall Luke using in on a handful of occasions, and none of them were good.

'Are you alright, Wiley?'

There was only silence on the other end of the line as Luke explained what had happened the previous evening.

'Leave it with me, and I will alert O'Donnell that you're coming in.'

Luke thanked her and the lift doors opened on the lobby level to spit Luke out into the mess that was not of his own making. As he walked towards the entrance, he could see an officer still speaking with the concierge and he hoped that they were already gathering one crucial piece of evidence.

'Have you pulled up the CCTV from last night?'

The officer shook his head.

'Believe it or not, there is no CCTV coverage of the entrance or the lift, Sir. Apparently the clientele of this particular tower are very protective of their privacy. There is only CCTV in the garage and that entrance door, and we are pulling that.'

Luke nodded grimly and left the officer to it. It was going to be an extremely long day.

Chief Superintendent Stephen O'Donnell probably waited for moments like this. Moments where DCI Wiley had screwed something up and O'Donnell could delight in revelling in it. As Luke made his way to the seventh floor of Scotland Yard, he could picture O'Donnell already — his chest puffed out and hands clasped behind his back, trying to suppress a grin but failing badly and not caring that Luke saw it.

But this had to be done. Luke needed to clear himself with his alibi and quickly as possible and head back to the scene. He knew that he was not responsible for Evie's death, but he did know that the fact he was the last person to be with her before her killer snatched her life away from her would bother him for a very long time.

He was going to find her killer and he was going to make him pay.

As Luke walked down the corridor towards O'Donnell's office, its was Rowdy who popped out of hers and stopped him, her hand outstretched in front of her like a traffic warden.

'He's already upstairs. You are to join him there.'

Luke knew immediately what this meant and while most of his colleagues would be riddled with anxiety at being summoned upstairs, he was not.

Upstairs was synonymous with Marina Scott-Carson, the

Commissioner of the Metropolitan Police Force. There was no one higher up to answer to, except the highest reaches of government.

'O'Donnell actually went up there voluntarily?' Luke asked.

'He was muttering profusely under his breath, so my guess is that he was — or he knew that you'd have to be sent up there eventually with this and he was being expedient,' Rowdy replied.

'Expedient? I highly doubt that.'

'Indeed.'

Rowdy didn't look particularly amused. Luke could tell that she was irritated with him.

'This isn't my fault, Rowdy.'

She raised her eyebrows.

'Okay,' she said. 'But you do have an incredible gift for being in the wrong place at the wrong time.'

'Tell me about it. Did you manage to get Sharma?'

'Of course I did,' Rowdy said.

Luke smiled and thanked her, just as the door to the emergency stairwell burst open with an almighty crack as it wasn't often used. Sharma burst through the door, out of breath and clutching a laptop under one arm and a mess of cords and adapters trailing behind him with the other.

Sharma saw Luke and Rowdy and grinned.

'You asked for me?' he said, still panting.

'A little bored down there, Sharma?' asked Rowdy.

'Well,' he said, trying to catch his breath but the smile on his face growing ever wider, 'covert policing is, you know, covert.'

'Don't get too excited,' Rowdy said. 'DCI Wiley has got himself in a bit of a pickle. Again. I'll let him fill you in. And then, Luke, get yourself upstairs.'

As if they had planned it in advance, Luke and Sharma both suddenly stood upright and saluted Rowdy.

'Oh for Christ's sake,' she hissed at them.

'Sharma, I do very much need your help and I need it quickly. A woman has been murdered — Evie Glover. She was discovered in her flat by her cleaning lady this morning. Dr. Chung and Hana are at the scene now and cause of death has yet to be determined, but time of death was approximately 9:30-11pm last night. I need you to forensically prove my whereabouts for that exact time frame.'

'Sir?' Sharma said, any joviality wiped off his face which now looked extremely concerned.

'I was with the victim last night at a grief support group and then for a cup of coffee afterwards.'

As he said this, Luke could see Rowdy soften.

'I need you to work your CCTV magic, Sharma. We should be visible on any Upper Street camera — the first one to check is on Town Hall east side. That will have the door on the adjacent building that we exited after leaving the grief support group. We walked down Upper Street towards Angel and went into a coffee shop on the west side — I'm sorry I don't remember what it was called but it was next to the theatre. If they have cameras in there, that would be great but I doubt they do. We left there at approximately 9pm and walked together down to City Road. She turned east to go home alone and you will find me continuing down towards Exmouth Market where I went into Enoki, the wine bar. I was in there until they closed at 11:30pm and got in an Uber home. I'll forward you the receipts.'

'Okay,' said Sharma. 'I got it. Don't worry.'

Luke began to walk towards the lift to head up to Marina Scott-Carson's office. He could feel Rowdy and Sharma staring at his back.

'At least the gang is back together,' he called out.

Ten

Hana really hated going through a crime scene when the victim was still present.

It was extremely difficult to concentrate.

Maybe there were some detectives who could shut off the part of them that felt deep sorrow for someone who had been killed and was now lying in front of them, but Hana was not one of them.

She had asked for Lombardi to take Luke's place because she needed another set of eyes to make sure they caught what she may be missing. And she needed a bit of support as well. Joy Lombardi was young but she was clever and capable and in that stage of her career where she sucked up everything like a sponge. Hana needed that next to her right now and she also just really liked Lombardi, which was saying something as Hana did not like that many people.

But Hana also knew that Lombardi would likely never have seen a crime scene as gruesome as this one, so she waited outside in the hallway of the tower just outside the door to Evie's flat and waited for her to arrive. The break was also good for Hana's hangover which was taking longer than she would have liked to subside.

When she stepped out of the lift, if Lombardi was nervous, she certainly wasn't showing it.

'DS Sawatsky,' she said. 'Thanks for asking for me.'

'You may want to hold that thought,' Hana said, handing her a pair of foot protectors and a set of latex gloves.

'And take your jacket off,' Hana said. 'You're suddenly going to feel hot when you step in here and you may feel nauseous. Deep breaths and if you need to step out, you just do it. Understood?'

'Got it.'

'Okay. Did Rowdy fill you in before you left?'

Lombardi shook her head.

'It seemed that details were a little scarce over at the unit.'

'The deceased is a woman named Evie Glover. She was quite brutally attacked and Dr. Chung is trying to get as much detail about her manner of death before the coroner takes her to the lab. We know that she attended a grief support group not far from here last night. She then had a coffee with DCI Wiley — don't ask — and we presume that she came straight home. We are looking for anything around the flat that sticks out. Let's get a sense of her and her life. Eyes open for anything — don't be shy to point out anything.'

'I'm ready,' said Lombardi.

Hana certainly hoped that was the case and they stepped through the door and into Evie's flat. Lombardi recoiled slightly at the odour, but tried not to show it. When they reached the body in the living room, the only sound was the shuffling of shoes all encased in their plastic covers and the artificial clicking sounds from digital cameras being used by the forensics team to capture every angle of the scene.

'Do we have any idea now of the cause of death?' Hana asked Dr. Chung.

'My best guess is exsanguination.'

'She bled out?'

'Most likely. The amount of blood here is astounding. But the killer toyed with her before that,' said Dr. Chung.

'How you do know?' asked Lombardi.

'Look at the marks on the floor. There was water here. It's mostly dried now — some will have been mixed with the blood which is why the streaks look fainter here than they should ordinarily be. Come with me into the bathroom.'

It would have been a gorgeous bathroom. Larger than it needed to be, calm cream marble tile on the floor, and a shower at one end that was so big, it didn't need a screen or a curtain. Water wasn't going to splash out of it — from either of the two shower heads on opposite sides and underneath tiled benches. There was a matching his and hers sink unit under a mirror that had adjustable light from just the touch of a button on its side. The other part of the bathroom housed the big, freestanding bathtub, the cedar bench next to it knocked over on its side.

It would have been a beautiful, calming space — more spa-like than utilitarian. Except it was covered in Evie's blood and the bottles of shampoo and conditioner and shaving cream had been thrown about; the glass toothbrush cups both smashed into pieces on the floor.

'He tried to drown her,' said Dr. Chung.

Lombardi walked over to the bathtub, which was empty apart from a ring of crimson around the white porcelain, about two thirds of the way up the side.

'How do you know?' she asked. 'There's no water in here.'

'Her eyes. There is slight hemorrhaging, but not enough to be the cause of death. I'll have a better idea when I get her back to the lab but I imagine there is a bit of water in the lungs, but she didn't drown.'

'What are you thinking, Lombardi?' asked Hana, as she

watched Lombardi circle the tub, crouch down to look at it and then stare around the rest of the bathroom. Hana knew what she thought, but she was testing Lombardi. If Lombardi knew this, she didn't let on. Or, Hana thought, she was struggling to vocalize what Hana suspected had happened in this flat last night.

Both Hana and Lombardi were picturing the horror of what had occurred in this bathroom just twelve or so hours earlier.

'He toyed with her,' Lombardi said. 'He pretended to drown her, and came very close, but then stopped.'

Lombardi wanted to continue, but had to stop speaking and take a small breath.

'Go on,' Hana encouraged.

'The killer wanted her to be terrified. He wanted control of her. Everything was about control. That's why after she was dead he came back and emptied the bath. He wasn't trying to hide evidence — her blood is still in the bathtub — but he wanted to control everything that happened last night.'

'I think you're right,' said Hana. 'The blood in this bathroom was incidental — he killed her in the living room. Then he came back here.'

Dr. Chung, usually only focused on the body in front of her, was also looking around the bathroom. Hana wondered for a moment if she was impressed by it.

'You'd think there would be more water everywhere in here, even if he cleaned up afterwards,' Dr. Chung said.

Hana was pretty sure that she had never before heard the medical examiner make any kind of comment about the crime scene that wasn't related to the evidence of the deceased. She was perplexed, but she was clearly also upset by the depravity of the killing.

'It's the floor,' Hana said softly. 'There is under floor heating in this bathroom. The water has evaporated. And that definitely means that she wasn't attacked with the weapon that led to her bleeding out in here. The blood wouldn't have evaporated.'

Hana could picture what the floor would have looked like had Evie bled out in the bathroom. It would have been a sticky, stained, gruesome mess.

The three women walked back into the living room where Evie lay alone on the sofa, the forensics team having moved into the bedroom to continue photographing the crime scene. Lombardi crouched down to get a better look at the body.

'Don't touch anything yet,' Hana cautioned, which made Lombardi flick her head back to look at Hana, clearly exasperated by the basic instruction.

'Sorry,' Hana muttered.

'Will you take forensic samples from her fingernails?' Lombardi asked Dr. Chung. 'A couple of them are broken.

'Yes. We will take forensics from her entire body, but you're thinking is correct here. She put up a hell of a fight. I would guess that you'll get decent DNA from her body and from any blood spatter in the bathroom. That won't be all hers.'

Hana was also staring at the body.

'When you get her back to the lab, I bet you will discover that she hasn't been sexually assaulted.'

There was no response from either Lombardi or Dr. Chung because all three women were thinking the exact same thing. There is no way that a soaking wet pair of jeans would have been able to have been put back, or pulled back up, on her body after such an assault.

'Somehow,' said Lombardi, 'that makes it worse. What on earth was the motivation?'

'I've been doing this a very long time,' said Dr. Chung. 'You'll discover the reason, but it won't ever make sense to you.'

A forensic officer entered the living room and cleared his throat.

'Excuse me, DS Sawatsky?'

'Yes,' said Hana.

'We'll still be another hour or so here, but I wanted to let you know that we have found a mobile phone in the bedroom.'

'Thank you,' said Hana, her voice sounding resigned.

'That's good, right?' Lombardi chipped in. 'Usually a killer would look to take the phone with him and dispose of it.'

She looked at Hana expectantly.

'Yes, it's a good thing,' Hana replied. 'I've got to make a quick call.'

Hana pulled out her own mobile phone and called into the Serious Crime Unit. It sounded to Lombardi that she was speaking to either Luke or Rowdy, and the call lasted only about a minute. When she hung up and slipped her phone back into her pocket, she gently shook her head towards Dr. Chung.

'What is it?' asked Lombardi, not understanding the unspoken communication between her two colleagues in the room.

'I just called into the unit to see if we have a next of kin yet,' said Hana. 'I'm afraid nothing popped up on any record.'

'Right,' said Lombardi, still not following.

Dr. Chung looked over at Evie and then walked over to the side of the living room where her equipment bag was propped up against the wall. She picked it up and pulled her latex gloves off, one by one, the pop of their release from her hands was the only sound in the room.

'I'll leave you two to it,' Dr. Chung said. 'I'll have the report for you by the end of the day.'

'Thank you,' Hana said, understanding that Dr. Chung

was about to clear her schedule and move any other impending work so she could focus on Evie Glover. And hopefully get them some answers.

The forensic officers asked if Hana and Lombardi would like the mobile phone brought to them and Hana nodded. When it was handed over, Hana held it delicately and Lombardi frowned slightly, wondering why they were being given the phone when it should be going straight into an evidence bag and rushed to the Serious Crime Unit so that Bobby Sharma could begin to work his magic on it.

'This part is always really hard,' Hana said. 'It has to be done, but somehow, it always gets to me.'

'What does?'

Lombardi watched with a combination of horror and fascination as Hana knelt down beside Evie's body and gently moved her head, brushing a strand of hair away from her face. Her eyes were open and bruising was beginning to appear on the left side of her face.

Hana clicked the button on the side of the phone to ensure the screen was alert and then held it in front of the dead woman's face. The phone unlocked and Hana quickly began scrolling through it.

'I didn't think you could do that,' said Lombardi.

'You'd be surprised,' Hana replied, still focused on the phone as she swiped through various screens. 'Her eyes didn't even need to be open. Most people don't have the "attention" function toggled on in their settings. She could have just been asleep and we would have been able to open the phone.'

'Right.'

'I know. It's gruesome and I dislike doing it. Dr. Chung can't bear it — that's why she left us to it. Do you know that the first thing I always look at is the camera roll? I always have this feeling that the last photo the victim has taken is of the killer.'

'Has that ever happened?' Lombardi asked.

'No.'

'But what do you need now before Sharma goes through the phone?'

Hana sighed and said, 'I got it.'

She held up the phone and showed Lombardi the screen. It was the contact screen for an entry named Mum.

Next of kin.

Eleven

For the second time in two days, Luke found himself staring at the hair of a woman sitting across from him and wondering how it looked like that and what is must have cost.

Marina Scott-Carson's hair was a shade of blonde that made her ageless. If you didn't look at her face, it could be the hair colour of a woman in her twenties, or it could be the perfect hue of a wealthy woman in her seventies. Scott-Carson didn't belong in either of these age categories — Luke guessed that she was probably around the sixty mark — and her perfectly coiffed jaw-length bob didn't seem to move. But it also didn't look like it had any hair product in it.

Luke respected Marina Scott-Carson, which was not something he could say about the man sitting next to her. O'Donnell was squirming in his chair ever so slightly. Luke could tell that he was trying to act like he was in charge of this situation and that he and Scott-Carson were on the same page, a united front about to interrogate Luke about how he was in this situation. But in reality, O'Donnell was squirming because he was intimidated by his boss and was frantic that this was all going to land on him.

And Luke knew that this was going to make for a particularly difficult time with O'Donnell as they tried to find Evie's killer, which was the last thing he needed.

There had been no pleasantries when Luke appeared at the door of the highest office in this building. Scott-Carson had barely glanced over at him, instead pointing to the chair in front of her. Luke had sat down in it and crossed his legs, then folded his hands in front of him rather like a naughty schoolboy waiting to be told off.

As he did this, he could almost see the steam coming out of O'Donnell's ears.

Not even a sigh emerged from Scott-Carson when she finally looked at Luke. Her face wasn't one of exasperation or anger, it looked like she simply didn't have time for this and maybe, just maybe, she was only a little bit bemused? It was hard to tell.

'Perhaps it would be a good idea to hear from your own lips, DCI Wiley, exactly what has transpired to bring you up to my office?'

'I get the feeling,' Luke said, 'that I should be apologizing for something that was, quite spectacularly, not my fault. It is dreadful what has happened to this woman.'

O'Donnell couldn't help himself. Without waiting for Scott-Carson to answer, he jumped in himself.

'And yet it always seems to be you that finds yourself in this kind of situation. You were barely back at work when a woman who had been murdered was found with a photograph of you in her pocket. Now you were on a date with a woman who is found murdered the very next day. Wrong place wrong time are we, Wiley?'

'I was not on a date,' Luke said, softly.

At this point Scott-Carson finally showed some sort of reaction and she closed her eyes.

'Who is the woman please and how do you know her?' Scott-Carson asked, her eyes still closed.

'Marina,' Luke said, the gesture of informality making her sit up, open her eyes and look at Luke.

'It is a coincidence that I met Evie Glover last night,' he continued, 'but I'm not sure that her death is one.'

Again, Scott-Carson didn't say a word and for once, O'Donnell joined her.

'I was at a group grief counselling meeting last night and Evie was there because her husband recently died. She sought me out after the meeting concluded and told me that she thought her husband had been murdered.'

'What was his cause of death?' O'Donnell asked.

'Suicide. He jumped over the balcony of their flat. Fourteenth floor.'

'The same flat she was found dead in this morning?' Scott-Carson said.

Luke nodded.

'What do we know about the husband?' Scott-Carson said, directing her question not at Luke but at O'Donnell.

O'Donnell's mouth opened like he had just been caught doing something he shouldn't have been doing and had no excuse. He stuttered out a series of guttural noises before stammering that the husband hadn't been under investigation for anything and this was the first they had heard of it.

'So we're starting from scratch,' Scott-Carson said.

'I'm afraid so,' Luke replied.

'Who do you have clearing your whereabouts last night? We have to be completely covered here — nothing, and I mean absolutely nothing, can come back on the Met in terms of protocol and your ability to be the lead detective on this.'

'Bobby Sharma should have me cleared within the hour,' Luke said, wondering if this was wildly optimistic.

'Good. Now I wish to speak to you alone,' Scott-Carson said.

Both Luke and O'Donnell remained in their seats.

'For Christ's sake, not you Stephen. Off you go.'

Luke suppressed the laughter that he could feel rising in his chest and if O'Donnell caught the twitch of his lips as he did this, he would make Luke pay for it later. O'Donnell didn't bother to close the door behind him as he left and Luke was surprised to watch Scott-Carson stand up from behind her desk and walk across her cavernous office to softly close it herself. She didn't return to her seat, but rather leaned against her desk in front of Luke, her long legs in her pencil skirt shimmering in black tights that were now at Luke's eye level, her ankles crossed so that her balance seemed to lie solely on the tip of one stiletto heel.

'How is DS Sawatsky getting on?' she asked.

'Hana? She's fine.'

'Any reason she was meeting with Philippa Nicolson last night?'

How on earth did Scott-Carson know this, Luke thought.

'I'm not really sure,' Luke said, marvelling slightly at the fact that this was the honest truth. 'I think Philippa happened to be in London and was checking in with Hana after her kidnapping ordeal.'

'And that was it?'

'Did you think otherwise?'

Marina Scott-Carson wasn't used to being answered with a question. It didn't happen particularly often at her rank, and she knew that Luke would play a game of who-knew-what if she continued to press him. Luke, on the other hand, was hoping that she would bite here because he suddenly wondered what Philippa Nicolson and Hana Sawatsky had really been discussing the previous evening.

'Get yourself cleared and back onto this case, DCI Wiley. God only knows why these things keep happening to you, but I can assure you that I do not have infinite patience.'

'No one would ever accuse you of that,' Luke said, getting out of her office as quickly as possible before anything else could be said.

Twelve

Luke had been close with his optimism. Sharma had managed to pull up CCTV and receipts that covered Luke's location from the time he left Evie Glover by Angel tube station to the approximate time of Evie's death and he did it in just under an hour and a half.

'What now, Sir?' Sharma had asked him, quite pleased with himself.

'Forensics is bringing in Evie's phone. Let's see what you can find.'

Hana and Lombardi were waiting for Luke at Evie's flat and he drove over there to take a quick look around himself before they had to notify the next of kin.

Forensics was still painstakingly going through each room and systematically taking samples of blood, photographing every inch of the space and looking for anything else that may have come from the body of the perpetrator. Hana and Lombardi were keeping mostly out of the way, but Luke could sense Hana's impatience when he arrived.

'That was quick,' she said when she saw Luke.

'Sharma's good,' Lombardi said, to no one in particular.

'Anything stand out so far?' Luke asked them.

Hana shook her head.

Everything in the flat looked normal. It was tidy enough, but not obsessively so, although probably a little cleaner than Hana would have kept it if the cleaning woman was due in the morning. The presence of Evie's husband was still everywhere in the flat and his death had clearly been enough of a shock that Evie hadn't even begun to think about removing his things.

'That's extremely fortunate,' Luke mused as he stared at the suit trousers hanging in the bedroom closet. They would need to begin to dig into Johnny Glover's past as well.

On the dining table in the main space, a table that looked like it had not been used or sat at in some time, was half a dozen condolence cards, propped up and open. Hana was photographing each one.

'We should speak to these people,' she said. 'Lombardi, will you see if Forensics is finished with the rubbish so that you can go through it. If we still have envelopes for these, that would speed things up.'

Lombardi hoped that the discarded envelopes might be in some sort of recycling receptacle so she didn't have to pick through the remnants of days old trash and headed down the hall to take a look.

'Evie let the killer in,' Luke said.

'Yes,' replied Hana, turning to look at what she had already seen in the kitchen.

On the counter were two wine glasses. They were the stemless kind and seemed like the only evidence in the flat that wasn't stained red.

'White wine,' Hana said. 'The rest of the bottle is in the fridge. They only had one glass as there's quite a bit left.'

Luke opened the fridge and scanned its contents. There wasn't much in there, supporting Evie's assertion that she had been staying with her sister for the past couple of weeks. Butter, a pint of milk that was past its use-by date, jars of pesto and jam and pre-chopped garlic. The wine was a decent bottle and probably not one that was picked up from the grocery store. Luke took a photo of the label and closed the fridge door.

'I think it's likely that Evie was not expecting her guest,' he said.

'One glass and then she asked him to leave and things got violent?'

'Maybe. But I don't like this at all. This killer isn't afraid of getting caught. His fingerprints will be on that wine glass, as will his DNA. His blood splatter will be in that bathroom.'

'I know. And something tells me that we are not going to get a match or a hit anywhere when the DNA and prints are run. This asshole is hiding in plain sight. I don't like it either.'

As Hana and Luke waited for Lombardi, Hana asked him to go over everything that Evie had said the previous night.

'I'm struggling to remember exactly,' Luke said.

'Why? You remember everything.'

She wasn't wrong, but Luke was so taken aback by the hour he spent with Evie — her insistence on having a coffee, the way she leaned towards him and whispered that she thought her husband was murdered — all of it had taken Luke so far out of his comfort zone that his brain wasn't taking everything in. He was too embarrassed to admit that he was really just trying to find a polite way to get the hell out of there. And now he felt a sharp pang of guilt.

'Okay, here's what I know,' he said, trying to itemize in his head everything that Evie Glover had said to him. 'Apart from what you already know — her husband Johnny died by falling over that balcony and Evie had been staying with her sister since it happened — she has a therapist who recommended the group grief counselling where I met her, and she said one other strange thing.'

'What?'

'We were talking about our spouses, you know, as you do when you've met because they have both died. I talked about how I met Sadie and when I asked Evie how she had met her husband, she said that she couldn't remember.'

'Maybe that was just her grief talking,' Hana said.

'No way. You don't forget how you met the love of your life. Something isn't right there.'

Lombardi poked her head back into the living room to let the detectives know that the corresponding envelopes to the condolence cards were nowhere to be found.

'It's okay,' said Hana. 'Sharma will be able to cross-reference from her phone contacts, I bet. Thanks for checking.'

'Would you like to join us while we do the next-of-kin notification?' Luke asked.

Lombardi shook her head and said that she'd like to continue to look through the scene with the Forensics team. Luke remembered that feeling as a young constable — wanting to see if he could spot what someone else had not.

Hana and Luke left Lombardi to it and headed down to the street level where the police cordon had finally been lifted and the detectives watched the residents and couriers and food delivery staff come and go out of the front entrance.

'There are too many people in this building,' Hana said. 'It's not helpful.'

'No,' Luke agreed. 'But maybe Evie Glover's mother can begin to tell us what we need to know.'

Thirteen

As Luke and Hana exited the apartment building on City Road, the man watched them and smiled. The male detective had looked right at him and hadn't seen anything that made him stop and take a closer look.

A rush of warmth flooded his body as it happened, as if he had just downed a shot of tequila.

You have no idea. I'm standing right here.

He checked his watch and saw that it was just past noon and his stomach was finally beginning to growl. The adrenaline in his body had taken this long to subside. His patience would have outlasted any hunger he felt anyway. He wanted to see who came running when he killed Evie. He wanted to see the moment a police car sped towards the building and stopped outside, its lights flashing while officers rushed inside. He had always wanted to witness this moment, but today was the very first time he knew it would happen. Evie had guaranteed it for him without even knowing.

Usually the body would lie undetected for hours — one time it took an entire weekend — before it was discovered. But

Evie had apologized for the messy bathroom when he popped in to use it.

'My cleaning lady is coming in the morning, so I didn't bother with it.'

As he relieved himself, he had looked around the bathroom, picturing what he would do to her here. He turned on the tap at the sink to wash his hands, but before he did so, he walked over to the bathtub, turned the knob to close the drain, and turned that tap on as well. He had held his hand under the stream of water and adjusted the temperature. Then he walked back to the sink and continued washing his hands, letting the bathtub continue to fill as he returned to Evie.

He had been surprised that she welcomed him into the flat without hesitation. Waiting for her downstairs, he had been sitting where he was sitting now — just across the street. Last night he had waited for her to settle in and when he saw a group of women all returning from drinks out, walk towards the front door of the tall, glass building, he jumped up and joined them just as they were opening the door. One of them turned to him and he flashed a smile and nodded at her, as if to thank her for holding the door open for him at just the right time.

He let them go up in the lift alone. Now that he was in the building, he could take his time. He knew there were no cameras in the building lobby and he knew when the concierge took his break.

He knew because he had been to this flat three weeks' earlier.

The glass of wine that was offered to him had been unexpected. He accepted it and they had talked in the living room for a little while. As Evie had drained the last of her glass, she had reached over as if to take his.

'Another?' she had said.

He hadn't answered but she took the glass from him anyway and put both of them on the kitchen counter. She turned around, still standing in the kitchen, and asked him the question that she had been waiting to ask. He realized that the wine was because she was nervous.

'Did you kill my husband?'

He wondered if she was going to run, or if she was going to scream. He knew from his previous visit that their next door neighbour lived abroad most of the time, but he was unsure about the rest of the flats on the floor.

He had stood up and walked towards the balcony, knowing that his fingerprints were already on the handle from his last visit, and that they would be on the wine glass and on the bathroom taps and probably on surfaces he couldn't remember touching.

He opened the balcony door and stepped out onto it. How ridiculous to have balconies at this height on a building in central London. The wind whipped through his hair and he thought that if Johnny had screamed when he went over that no one would have been able to hear him.

As he stood there, he reached down to touch the object that was in the front pocket of his jeans. His pocket knife.

It was the only thing from his childhood that he had kept and he rubbed it through the denim fabric, as he had done all those years ago on the night when he became who he now was.

The pocket knife had been a gift that had been opened on Christmas Day. But it was not a gift for him.

He had watched his brother open it.

It wasn't even his brother. They weren't biologically related. They had been forced together by the marriage of two narcissist parents. He and his sister were suddenly pulled out of their home, their own mother losing a custody battle in court, and they were dropped into another house in another county with a new mother who hated them. And her child, a son, hated them even more.

He was forced to call this boy, who was five years older than him, his brother.

On that Christmas morning, the first one they had spent together in their new blended family. the gifts under the tree were piled high and were carefully wrapped. He had been excited and at ten years old, when Christmas magic should be waning a bit, the scene in the living room in front of him was festive and full of promise.

But then the gifts began to be opened. There was one or two for him, and the same for his sister. The rest were all for his new older brother. But the worst part? It was his own father, who had carefully chosen the gifts for his *new* son. His own father who smiled and wrapped his arm around this boy who was practically a stranger.

All the while his new mother beamed in a way that made him feel sick. The power she had over his father. It turned his stomach.

The small box, its wrapping paper folded precisely with clear sellotape, was left purposely until the very end of the gift opening. His brother ripped it open and even he was in awe of the object in the box.

A silver pocket knife.

His brother turned it over delicately in his hands. He pulled out each little perfect tool. The screwdriver, the scissors, the toothpick, the saw, the corkscrew.

The large flat, sharp blade.

He had never before coveted something as much as he coveted that pocket knife.

The night that it became his was in many ways the night that led to this one.

On the balcony, he visualized what he was about to do. He

hoped that Evie would not join him outside on the balcony because he would be too tempted to simply push her over the edge. But after her husband's death, she didn't dare come outside.

Especially with him standing there.

Fourteen

Evie Glover's mother lived in the leafy suburbs of south London where the houses are all detached and have gardens out both the front and the back. It was a neighbourhood that you might call bucolic and Hana and Luke could both sense the slightly cleaner air as they stepped out of the car.

There had been no address for Evie's mother stored in her phone, so Luke had made the call to break the news that would shatter her life. When they asked for the address and discovered that it was in London, the detectives drove directly there.

Luke had recommended that she call a friend to come to the house and sit with her until they arrived, but they didn't see any other car parked outside her house.

'Maybe she called a neighbour,' said Hana as they approached the front door.

There was no doorbell, only a large door knocker in the shape of a fox head. Luke lifted it and rapped as quietly as he thought he could get away with and then stepped back.

It took a good minute before the door swung open and

Evie's mother was clearly in shock. She was around sixty, in great shape, in a pair of jeans and a long cashmere sweater that was expensive, but probably only worn around the house. A small hole was visible just below the neckline, the work of a hungry moth.

Hana looked at the woman's eyes and they were bright and wide, no sign of redness or puffy skin. She had yet to cry.

'Mrs. Loughbrough? I'm Detective Chief Inspector Luke Wiley, and this is my partner, Detective Sargeant Hana Sawatsky. I'm the person who called you earlier today with this terrible news. We are deeply sorry for your loss.'

'Come in.'

Evie's mother waited until both detectives were inside and then shut the door behind them.

'Won't you follow me?' she said, moving through the large entrance hall into a sitting room that ran off it.

There was a tray of tea, all set up and waiting for them. Four cups and saucers, a teapot, sugar and milk, four teaspoons. A plate of biscuits.

'I wasn't sure how many people were coming,' Evie's mother said, rubbing her forearms in what Hana guessed was a nervous habit.

Luke stared at the tea tray thinking that of all of the houses and flats and workplaces he had visited to speak to a recently bereaved relative, this was a first. Either this news was such a shock that she didn't know what else to do with herself and her time as she was waiting for the detectives to arrive.

Or this news wasn't a shock at all.

'That's very kind,' Luke said. 'I'm going to sit here and Hana would you mind pouring? Please, Mrs. Loughbrough, have a seat. We can talk you through what we know and then I'm afraid that we are going to have a lot of questions.'

'May,' said Evie's mother.

'Sorry?'

'My name is May. Please call me May. I'm divorced, but somehow I kept my ex-husband's ridiculous last name.'

'Right,' said Luke. 'Would you like us to contact him for you?'

'No, that's not necessary. He died a few years ago. Thank god. This would have killed him.'

Hana handed Luke a cup of tea, which he promptly put down on the table. She poured another cup for herself, and one for May and pushed the tray towards her so she could add her own milk and sugar. May waved her off. Hana knew that this was the moment the news was beginning to sink in. Her daughter was dead.

May's breathing began to stutter and the tears began to form.

'What exactly happened?' she managed to squeak out, before gripping the edge of the sofa beneath her.

'Evie was found this morning at home by her cleaning lady at approximately 8:30am. She had been killed. We are unsure of the exact cause of death, but we will let you know as soon as our medical examiner has concluded their work.'

'Where was she?'

'She was on the sofa in her living room,' Hana said. 'I'm very sorry.'

'The first question I have is an obvious one, but please do take your time and think about it. You may also think of something later and at any point, you should call us. No detail is too small and we are always happy to hear from you. Do you know of anyone who would wish to harm your daughter?' Luke asked.

May took a deep breath and her face was one of complete anguish, like if she could just come up with the right name then all of this would go away. As if she could erase the horror of what she was being asked to think about.

'I'm not sure. I'm sorry. I just cannot believe this has happened.'

Hana took a sip of the very strong tea and placed her cup back in the saucer.

'There was no sign of a forced entry into the flat, so our working assumption at the moment is that Evie knew who killed her.'

'I can't believe this is happening. Who would do this to her?'

'When was the last time you spoke to Evie?' Hana asked, knowing full well that it was yesterday morning from Evie's phone log.

'Yesterday,' May said. 'She had called to say good morning. I mean, there was no reason for the call. She often rang out of the blue to check in on me.'

'And she didn't say what she was getting up to yesterday? Anything at all about how she was spending her day?'

'I don't think so.'

Luke had been waiting to ask about Evie's husband, hoping that May would volunteer a connection between the two deaths, but none seemed forthcoming.

'We understand that Evie's husband died about three weeks ago. Is that correct?'

May nodded her head.

'Yes, he died by suicide. We only just attended his service.'

Both Luke and Hana noticed that there didn't seem to be any hint of emotion about Johnny's death coming from Evie's mother. But perhaps she was simply too exhausted by two deaths to elicit more emotion than was currently on display to the detectives.

'May, I have what could seem like an odd question,' Luke said. 'But do you think there is any chance that Evie's husband did not take his own life? That perhaps he was purposely killed?'

At this question, May's head snapped up and her jaw clicked and she opened her mouth as if to shout something. It was a reaction that made both Luke and Hana start slightly.

'That man,' she hissed. 'That man was the cause of all of this.'

'What do you mean?'

'Evie should never have married him. Johnny had nothing to offer her. I told her that when they got engaged and she never forgave me for it. But he was a waste of her time.'

'Can you tell us a little more about him?' Hana asked.

At this question, May Loughbrough laughed. The marks of the tears that had slid down her face were still visible and she wiped them away. The poor woman seemed to be a complete mess of emotion.

'There isn't much to tell. He was a weak man. It was no surprise to me that he killed himself. I'm not ashamed to say that I felt a sense of relief when it happened. I felt that Evie was finally going to get her life back.'

'What do you mean that Johnny was a weak man?' Hana prompted.

'He had a group of friends when Evie met him. They thought that life was one big party and Johnny went along with it all. When Evie got involved, we never saw her and then all of the sudden she was getting married. We thought it was going to ruin her life and now this has happened. She is dead.'

'Are you saying that you think one of these friends may have been involved?' Luke asked.

'I have no idea,' Evie's mother said, beginning to cry once again. 'I don't think she saw them anymore. She said that they had all lost touch and that even Johnny wasn't seeing them. But after this, I'm not sure what I believe.'

Luke and Hana looked at each other, unsure where to go with this information that, although helpful, without specifics, was going to be a mess to wade through to get some real answers.

'We understand that after Johnny's death, Evie was staying with her sister? Do you think that she may have more information? Have you let her know what has happened?' asked Luke.

May Loughbrough looked confused by the question and said nothing. Luke gently repeated it. As he did so, the sinking feeling in Hana's stomach was a familiar one.

'I don't understand. What do you mean? Evie doesn't have a sister.'

'I'm sorry?' Luke said.

'Evie doesn't have a sister. Evie is an only child.'

Fifteen

Dr. Chung knew that everyone at the Met thought she was unflappable. She thought this about herself as well and she considered it one of her best qualities. You had to have this kind of persona in her position. To spend day after day at a crime scene and then hour after hour in the lab with the deceased took a lot of perseverance, a lot of patience, and a strong stomach.

But somehow Evie Glover was getting to her.

She wasn't used to this feeling.

Evie's body had yet to arrive when Dr. Chung returned to her lab in the bottom of New Scotland Yard. She was anxious, another unusual feeling, so she had gone for a brisk walk down the Embankment. Although it was lunchtime, eating would have been impossible.

Spring was just around the corner in London and you could feel the promise of it in the air. It was still cool enough to need a scarf, especially by the river, but Dr. Chung was grateful for both the fresh air whipping across her face and the bright sky that reflected the light of the water back towards her.

Why was she so shaken by her morning?

Dr. Chung had attended hundreds of crime scenes, many much worse than this one. Was it something to do with Evie in particular? She was a good ten years older than her own daughter, so it wasn't that. There was nothing else particularly remarkable about her.

Maybe that was it.

Maybe it was the unremarkable nature of this young woman and the brutal way in which she was killed that was affecting her.

No one deserved what she had gone through.

As she walked towards Hungerford Bridge, she tried to clear her head. She needed to not have any preconceived idea about what had happened to Evie Glover in her flat. She needed to wipe the crime scene out of her memory. But this wasn't going to be easy. It had been an almighty mess, but what was haunting her was the fact that the objects in the flat weren't smashed and broken. Apart from the toothbrush cup in the bathroom, everything seemed in place. The cushions on the sofa were still atop the carefully folded blanket. The condolence cards were still upright on the table. The television remotes were lined up on the console table and every framed poster and painting on the wall was hanging in its proper place, perfectly straight.

Dr. Chung knew from the initial examination of the body at the scene that Evie Glover had fought her attacker. But the drained bathtub and the ordered flat meant one thing.

After she was dead, the killer had taken his time and rearranged anything that had been knocked out of place. She could picture him standing there making sure that the flat looked like it always did.

He knew the flat.

He knew her.

And he wasn't afraid of being caught.

She walked as far as Waterloo Bridge and then turned around when her phone vibrated in her pocket, alerting her that Evie Glover had arrived at the lab. As she turned around and headed back, she knew that she was going to break one of her cardinal rules that evening. She never took her work home with her. Physical files, yes — emotional reactions, never. Dr. Chung had a little home office and often worked into the evening, mostly the tedium of writing reports and dictating notes. The Met was an interesting place to work, but the bureaucracy was never-ending.

She always locked the files away in her desk drawer, careful to keep her work, and especially the photographs of the dead, away from her husband and her children. But she also was mindful of locking away the mental toil of dealing with the work of the depraved. It was her choice to work in this position, to decide to continue in this particular job, but listening to the details of it, was not her husband's choice.

She knew that he respected what she did, but she also knew that he was grateful that he did not have to hear about it.

But very occasionally, she would tell him about her day. She would tell her husband about the person on the slab in front of her and the findings of the autopsy she had performed. She would wring her hands as she told him and she would apologize, but sometimes this was the only thing she knew to do in the rare moments when the job overwhelmed her.

Her husband would listen and nod and not say much in response, but when they crawled into bed at the end of the evening, he would pull her close and stroke her hair. Sometimes she would cry. Tonight would probably be one of those nights.

But now she pushed all of these feelings to the side and she washed her hands as she returned to the lab. Her assistant had prepared her instruments in the tray in the exact order she liked them and he had boiled the kettle and placed a green teabag in the mug next to it.

She was especially grateful for this gesture, as if her assistant knew that this particular examination was going to be difficult. She pulled on her lab coat and scrolled through the music app on her phone. Dr. Chung liked to listen to instrumental jazz while she worked and as she pressed play, she squeezed her hands into her gloves and pulled back the sheet covering Evie Glover.

Her clothes had been removed by the Forensics Team and this was the first time Dr. Chung could see the entire body.

Her eyes scanned every part of her and Dr. Chung crouched down close to the body without touching her, taking in every bruise, every contusion, every incision the killer had made.

Then she saw it.

Something that definitely shouldn't be there.

She leaned in closer, her fingertips brushing the skin ever so slightly.

Then she reached for her camera.

Luke was sure that he had missed something. He was going over in his head every minute of the hour he spent with Evie.

'Tell me again absolutely everything Evie said to you last night.'

Hana was quizzing Luke on the previous evening and it really wasn't helping.

'I've told you everything already, Hana. She said she was staying with her sister. I didn't mishear her. She was very clear.'

'But that's what I'm getting at. If she was that clear with you, it has to mean something. Why would she seek you out, tell you that she was convinced her husband was murdered and then lie about where she had been staying? She wouldn't even have brought it up.'

'I don't know.'

'Who are you texting?'

'Sharma. I'm want to know if there is something on Evie's phone.'

'I'm sorry, are we playing a game of cryptic crossword here? Do you want to tell me what's going on?'

'One second,' Luke said.

Hana swerved lanes and the car she cut in front of honked its horn, then slowed down and waved an apology when he realized it was an unmarked police car.

'Feel like getting back to the Met a little quicker?' Hana said, moving her hand towards the button that would switch on the lights and siren.

'Hold on,' Luke said, placing his own hand gently on top of Hana's, but still staring at his phone screen.

'Shit,' he said. 'Just drive towards the Met, but we may be veering off. I need to make a call.'

Luke scrolled through his contacts and found the name he was looking for and pressed the dial button. He didn't expect there to be an answer but after a couple of rings, his therapist answered. He made a split second decision and pressed the bluetooth button to connect the phone to the car.

'Hi, Nicky? It's Luke and you are on speaker. Hana is here with me.'

There was a moment of silence as his therapist was determining why Luke was calling in the middle of the day and why the call was on speaker with his detective partner listening in.

'Yes, Luke,' Nicky said, understanding that something was very wrong.

'Nicky, this call isn't being recorded, but I have Hana here as a witness to everything I am saying. Just in case.'

Hana had just clued into why Luke was making this call and she looked at him and nodded, slowing down the car.

'Good afternoon Nicky, this is DS Hana Sawatsky. Luke will fill you in on what is happening.'

Nicky did not reply, leaving space as she always did in Luke's sessions for her patient to fill in the gaps.

'Nicky, I need you to keep this as confidential information because we have not released anything to the public or the media. This does not involve you directly, but I'm afraid it does involve me.'

'I understand,' Nicky said.

'At the group counselling meeting last night, one of the attendees was Evie Glover. She was discovered this morning at home and we have deemed it a homicide. I spoke to her at length last night. She said that her therapist had recommended her to the counselling and we are going to need that therapist's name.'

Once again there was silence on the other end of the line. Luke was used to this, but Hana was not. Although she was driving, she kept glancing over at Luke, wondering why he was not reacting, then she peered at her dashboard to see if the bluetooth connection had been lost.

Luke knew that Nicky would be taking in this information and having no external reaction whatsoever. He knew that his therapist would be turning his words over and over in her head and considering exactly how to respond, with every word being carefully chosen. But what came out of Nicky's mouth was completely unexpected.

'Luke, I am Evie's therapist.'

Sixteen

Lombardi was standing in the Incident Room on the seventh floor of Scotland Yard and smiling to herself. The white board had been set up at the front of the room and Rowdy had already found the espresso machine and placed it on the table in the corner. It had been a few weeks since she had stood in here and although it was about to get tense and frenetic and she wondered how much sleep she would be getting over the next few days, she was happy to be standing there.

'I'm not sure that grinning in the Incident Room is the best look.'

Sharma was at the door, two laptops under one arm and a tangled bundle of cables and boxes marked 'Sensitive' in the other.

'Give me a hand?' Sharma said.

Lombardi grabbed the laptops from him and took them over to his usual table.

'You know what? I think I might take this table.'

'DS Sawatsky usually sits on that one,' Lombardi said.

'Let's see if she gives me a pass this time. I'd like a different view.'

Lombardi couldn't help but snort at that comment. The view of the stark white walls of the Incident Room and the occasional scuff mark from the tables that have been shoved against them for the past decade was pretty much the same wherever you sat in there.

'How've you been?' she asked.

'Fine. A little bored, to be honest. They've had me on Covert Policing on the fifth floor, which I initially thought was a great assignment after the London Sniper Case.'

'It wasn't?'

'Not even close. They call it 'covert' for a reason. The reason being you can't actually know what you're analyzing. It was like I was piloting a plane completely blind.'

'We're pilots now?' Lombardi said.

'Well, you know what I mean,' Sharma replied, a little sheepishly.

Lombardi was pleased to see Bobby Sharma. They had worked together on a couple of cases before the London Sniper, but on that case, they had been teamed up and had spent many days working quite closely. Lombardi wasn't going to admit it, but she had missed him after they had caught the killer and were re-assigned from the Serious Crime Unit.

She noticed that Sharma had let his stubble grow in a little bit and she wondered if he had been overworked and hadn't had time to shave, or if he had let it grow on purpose. It suited him.

'Do you have a lot of detail on what we're dealing with yet? I've been working on only one thing for the past couple of hours,' Sharma said.

'What were you working on?'

'Believe it or not — DCI Wiley's alibi.'

'Yes, I heard a little bit about that. I was at the crime scene with DS Sawatsky. You cleared that up pretty quickly.'

'Thanks,' Sharma said, smiling at her and then quickly looking down at his laptops, busying himself with plugging everything in.

'What was the crime scene like?' Sharma asked.

Lombardi didn't quite know how to answer this. Both she and Sharma were used to seeing photographs and files of forensic data when it was presented to them in the Incident Room. They had interviewed witnesses and canvassed areas around a crime scene, but before this morning, Lombardi had never found herself smack in the middle of one.

If she was being honest, she had been overwhelmed by it.

'It was tough' she said, hesitating about what exactly to say. 'I mean, I've never experienced something like that before. It was brutal. The scene was horrific.'

Sharma stopped fiddling with the cables and electronic jammers that prevented his data from being scanned anywhere except within the Met building, and looked at Lombardi. He didn't say anything, waiting for her to continue. Part of him was fascinated, and the rest of him felt sympathy for her. He wasn't sure that he would cope particularly well in the thick of the actual gore of a murder scene.

'Was the body still there?'

Lombardi nodded.

'She had been brutally attacked. And it looked like she fought for her life.'

'We'll get him,' Sharma said.

'Yeah,' Lombardi replied, composing herself. 'We'll get him.'

Sharma offered to make her a coffee, but Lombardi declined after checking the time on her phone. Even if she got out of here at any kind of decent time, if she had caffeine this late in the afternoon, there was zero chance that she'd get any sleep.

'Was it difficult to piece together DCI Wiley's alibi?'

'Luckily, no. He knew exactly where he was and exactly what camera would have picked him up. Plus he had some receipts from the bar he was in with Sawatsky. It was pretty easy to pull everything quickly.'

Lombardi lowered her voice for her next question.

'What was DCI Wiley doing....exactly?'

'What do you mean?'

'Well,' said Lombardi. 'He was with the victim. Wiley and Sawatsky weren't going to fill me in on the details, were they?'

'Oh god,' said Sharma. 'They didn't explain the context to me. Just that I had to confirm Wiley's whereabouts. They didn't say that the woman he was with was the victim. Oh my *god*.'

'Stop saying that,' Lombardi said. 'What the hell did you see on the CCTV?'

'I assumed they were on a date.'

'No.'

'Yes. That's what it certainly looked like.'

'There's no way,' Lombardi shook her head. 'His wife has just died. He's clearly still devastated. There is no way he was on a date last night.'

'Do you want to see for yourself?'

Lombardi opened her mouth to reply. Of course she wanted to see the video. But she also respected Luke too much to say yes. And she felt bizarrely protective of him.

'Look,' said Sharma. 'I still have it up here.'

He swivelled one of his laptops towards her and for a split second Lombardi turned to look away. But the image on the screen was too mesmerizing.

There was Luke in the cafe sitting across from Evie Glover. Both of them looked relaxed, their posture easy and natural. They weren't the focus of the camera image, which had captured several tables at the cafe, but if you had been watching this footage unaware of what was going to happen to this woman in just a matter of hours, you would still be staring only at them.

They did look like they were on a date.

Without the benefit of sound, Sharma and Lombardi could only guess what the two of them were saying to each other. When Evie said something and Luke reacted with laughter, they watched him lean forward towards Evie and reply.

Lombardi and Sharma couldn't help but lean towards the laptop screen themselves, as if they were eavesdropping.

A voice shattered their concentration.

'Busy confirming DCI Wiley's abili again, are we?'

Laura Rowdy had a face like thunder, standing at the doorway to the Incident Room.

Sharma slapped the laptop shut and Lombardi turned to glare at him. They had looked guilty enough.

'O'Donnell wants to brief both of you before Wiley and Sawatsky return. So off you go.'

Lombardi and Sharma said nothing and quickly scampered out the door and down the hallway to be subjected to whatever wrath O'Donnell wished to dole out that afternoon. Rowdy walked towards the door and closed it softly, before returning to Sharma's laptop.

She opened it and bypassed his security setting with her own. The image of Luke and Evie Glover reappeared on the screen. Rowdy pressed the play button and began to screen the footage. She watched Evie reach over and brush something off Luke's sleeve. Pressing pause, and then rewind, Rowdy watched the footage again.

Her mobile began to ring and Rowdy looked towards the door before gently closing Sharma's laptop.

'Laura,' said the voice on the other end of the line. 'It's Chung. Are Luke and Hana back yet? I need them to see something.'

Seventeen

Luke was very quiet on the drive back to Scotland Yard. When they had hung up from Dr. Nicky Bowman, he hadn't said anything.

For once, Hana wasn't sure what he was thinking.

'What's up?' she said, weaving her way through south London traffic towards the river.

'I'm irritated.'

Hana couldn't help but laugh.

'I'm sorry? Why?'

'Nicky is my therapist.'

'Luke, she's not exclusively yours. You know that right? She has a whole raft of clients.'

Luke sighed.

'Yes, of course I know that. That's not my point. The point is that Nicky specifically recommended this group grief counselling to me, knowing full well that she had another client of hers attending it. We were bound to meet.'

'And?'

'And...'

Luke trailed off, not actually having a point and unsure as

to why he felt so upset about this revelation. Did he feel suddenly less important as a client? Was he somehow blaming Nicky for what had happened to Evie Glover? That was a preposterous thing to think.

'Never mind,' Luke said. 'Let's just leave it.'

Luke and Hana had arranged to meet with Nicky at her home later that evening, once she had finished her day with her clients. Luke told himself that he needed to sort through his emotions about this before they saw her. He needed to be able to focus.

When the detectives arrived at Scotland Yard, they entered with their security passes and did not get into the lift for the seventh floor at the Serious Crime Unit. Instead, they walked past the lifts and through the emergency exit door that they knew would take them on a short cut to the underground section of the building where Dr. Chung's lab was located.

The faint sound of instrumental jazz could just be heard over the clicking of their shoes on the concrete floor. One of the overhead fluorescent lights flicked on and off.

'I don't know why they had to make it so creepy down here. It's like a horror movie,' said Hana.

Luke turned around to give her a look and then continued down the hall. When they reached Dr. Chung's office, they poked their heads inside but it was empty.

'She must still be in the lab,' Luke said.

Following the music, they reached the small laboratory at the end of the hallway. Evie Glover was on the metal table in the centre of the room, covered with a sheet. Dr. Chung was sitting on a stool in the corner, sipping a mug of tea and staring at her.

'Dr. Chung,' Luke said in greeting. 'You wanted to see us?'

Hana looked at the doctor and saw that she was tired. It wasn't physical exhaustion that was etched on her face, but something deeper — the result of being bombarded by the capacity for cruelty by another human being.

'This one is getting to me,' Dr. Chung said.

'I know,' Hana replied, and she shut the door to the hallway, as if to protect the four of them in this room from whatever evils were lurking just outside.

Luke knew from experience that Dr. Chung wouldn't have called him and Hana in if there wasn't something that didn't seem right with the victim. But he also knew that as methodical as she was, they were going to have to let her talk them through the entirety of her findings.

'Shall we begin?' Dr. Chung said, easing herself off the stool and putting down her mug.

She walked over to Evie's body and tucked a strand of her hair behind her ear.

'This poor girl was put through the wringer. My initial guess was correct. The actual cause of death of exsanguination — from this incision here.'

Dr. Chung pointed to a small cut on her neck.

'That doesn't look like a massive wound,' said Hana.

'It's not. It's quite deep, though. And I don't believe that she was conscious when the killer made it. There is no evidence of tearing around the wound or other scratches on her neck or torso. She didn't resist the cut that killed her.'

Thank god, both detectives thought to themselves.

'And the big question?' Luke said.

'No. She was not sexually assaulted,' Dr. Chung replied. 'No bruising or any sign at all that she had sex in the past few days.'

Dr. Chung had been correct about the attempted drowning in the bathtub. There was some residual water found in the lungs, but nothing more than swallowing water as you would have done in a swimming pool while larking around as a child.

The killer hadn't strangled her, but had held her down by her torso which was the part of her body that showed the most bruising apart from the left side of her face and her left hip.

'I think he dragged her from that side,' Dr. Chung said, 'her shoulder is dislocated. It would have been extremely painful.'

'What makes you think that she was conscious for that part?' Luke asked.

'Her lips, her tongue and the inside of her cheeks are swollen where she has bitten them. You don't do that when you are drowning. You only do that if you are in indescribable pain.'

'Jesus,' whispered Hana, staring at Evie's face, feeling a dangerous combination of sympathy and fury.

'I know,' Dr. Chung said. 'I'm not going to be able to get this one out of my head for some time. But that's not why I called you down here.'

Luke and Hana looked at her expectantly.

'It's this.'

Dr. Chung pulled the sheet back and the skin tone of Evie's naked body almost exactly matched its stark white colour. She pointed to Evie's hip bone which seemed pronounced in death, jutting up towards them. Luke and Hana crouched down to see what Dr. Chung was pointing at.

About an inch from the hip bone was a scratch. The detectives peered at it and realized that it wasn't an accidental wound. The incision was small, only about one centimetre, but it was deep and would have been made by a sharp blade.

The cut was in the shape of a V.

'There's something about the V that really made me look at it,' Dr. Chung said. 'The lines at the bottom of the V don't quite match up perfectly, but it's very close. Whoever did this wasn't haphazardly scrawling the shape of a V into her. This was methodical. He wanted to take his time.'

'Was she alive when this was done?' Hana asked.

'It must be impossible to tell,' Luke added.

'No. I'll be able to determine that. It's a biological test that I can run using histamines and serotonin and it will show whether this incision was antemortem or postmortem. I should be able to determine the time frame within 5-15 minutes of her death, if that was the case.'

'You're amazing,' said Hana, being completely serious.

'It's just science, Sawatsky.'

'What do you think this means?' Luke said aloud to no one in particular, in the way he often posed questions to his colleagues that were really just the ones in his own head.

'Maybe it's the killer's initial,' said Hana. 'Wouldn't that be convenient.'

'Wouldn't it,' said Dr. Chung, pulling the sheet back up over Evie and returning to her mug of lukewarm tea.

'Have you sent photos of all of this up to the Incident Room?' Luke said.

Dr. Chung nodded.

'Yes, Sharma confirmed receipt. You have everything you need up there. I hope you understand why I asked you to look at Evie's wound in person.'

Hana stepped over to Dr. Chung and placed her hand on the medical examiner's arm.

'We do. Don't worry, we'll get him.'

As the detectives stood in the lift that was taking them from the bowels of the building up to the seventh floor, Luke rubbed his jaw.

'What is it?' Hana asked him, attuned to his little ticks that meant he was either thinking something he wasn't sharing or was concerned about something.

'You don't usually give out assurances,' he said. 'That's all.'

'What can I say,' said Hana as the lift doors opened. 'This one has got to me, too.'

Walking into the Incident Room and seeing it set up and buzzing already made both detectives take a deep breath and truth be told, the sight provided a bit of comfort for both of them as well. What that said about them was something that they would push aside for the moment as they got to work.

'Sharma, many thanks for clearing me so quickly this morning,' Luke said as he made a beeline to the espresso machine.

'No problem, Sir,' he replied.

'DS Sawatsky, I've been filing the photographs taken by Forensics per room and have them ready to go,' said Lombardi, looking up from her laptop.

'Thanks. And good work this morning at the scene. I know that wouldn't have been easy. It was a particularly tough one,' said Hana.

Lombardi appreciated the vote of confidence and also felt relieved to know that the gruesome nature of Evie's flat wasn't what she would be seeing on a regular basis.

Luke sipped his coffee and asked Sharma to pull up the images from Dr. Chung's autopsy.

'We've just come from the lab and Dr. Chung ran us through the autopsy and cause of death. Evie Glover bled out from a careful incision to her jugular,' he said. 'But she also pointed out something unusual. Everyone, take a look at this.'

Luke was leaning over Sharma as the images of Evie's body flashed up on Sharma's laptop.

'There, that one. Can you mirror it to the screen up front please?'

Luke spotted Rowdy hovering at the door to the Incident Room and he beckoned her inside. She stepped in and closed the door behind her. Sharma looked up and smiled, slightly sheepishly at her. Rowdy did not react.

But Lombardi had not noticed that Rowdy had entered the room. She was staring intently at the image on the screen in front of her. Lombardi stood up and walked towards it, taking a closer look.

'What is it?' Hana asked.

'I know this,' she said. 'I just saw this.'

The rest of the team watched Lombardi as she rushed to her laptop and began scrolling through the images from Forensics. She was muttering under her breath.

Suddenly Lombardi stood up again. She looked to the screen at the front of the room, the V carved into Evie Glover's flesh magnified to at least fifty times its size, a haunting spectre reflected in her glasses as she approached it.

'Sharma,' she said. 'Put up the image from my laptop, too.'

He reached over and clicked the mouse on her laptop creating two images side by side on the screen.

On the left was the slightly imperfect V on Evie's body. On the right was a flyer with a logo that contained the exact same letter, it's downward point equally imperfect.

Eighteen

It was particularly strange for Luke to be standing on Dr. Nicky Bowman's front porch, waiting for her to answer the door, with Hana standing right next to him.

Hana, on the other hand, had been looking forward to this moment all afternoon. Even though it had been her recommendation that led Luke to her therapist, Hana had never actually met Nicky. She had simply come highly recommended from an old colleague in the army and if that person had been able to tolerate this particular therapist, she knew that Luke would also be able to speak to her.

She had never said anything to Luke, but she had been secretly smug for the past year that he continued to see her and clearly got on with her extremely well.

Until today, maybe.

'Is this weird?' Hana said to him.

Luke didn't answer, which was enough of an answer for Hana.

The door opened and there stood Dr. Nicky Bowman. She looked almost exactly like Hana thought she would, although she had expected tortoiseshell glasses for some reason, and Nicky wasn't wearing glasses.

Nicky was tall and slim and had let her hair go prematurely grey for her age. Hana guessed that she was barely the other side of fifty, and she was dressed in black jeans, black Chelsea boots and a forest green mock neck wool sweater.

'Come in, please,' she said, letting the detectives inside and then closing the door behind them.

Nicky began to walk upstairs and they followed her. Luke could see Hana doing what he did the very first time he walked through Nicky's front door — take in every detail about the house that she could. What could she learn from her brief vantage point that encompassed part of the kitchen, the dining room table in the open plan space and a hint of the living room beyond it.

Quite a lot.

It was just after seven o'clock in the evening and although a partner could still be making their way home from their workplace, the house had the feeling that only one person lived there. And Hana could tell a mile away if there was a man living somewhere, which clearly was not the case here.

The art on the wall in the dining room consisted of about a dozen differently sized framed prints and oil canvases. While they were curated and carefully placed on the wall, these looked like pieces that had been collected over many years and many travels.

Hana felt a small wave of sadness, imagining that whoever Nicky collected these with was no longer here.

But this was not her business and it was not why she was at Luke's therapist's house this evening. She had to also keep reminding herself that Dr. Nicky Bowman was also Evie Glover's therapist and now Evie was dead.

Nicky showed them into her office at the top of the first

flight of stairs in a warmly lit room that overlooked the street. Luke went to sit where he usually did and then stopped. It didn't feel right. He wasn't here to discuss his own internal world and he certainly wasn't here for support. He sat on a chair that was diagonal to Nicky, and where he had never sat before. Hana went and unknowingly took his usual place on the sofa.

Nicky did not say anything, waiting for the detectives to instigate the conversation. Luke was the one who spoke first.

'Nicky, this is obviously a little different. Have you ever been interviewed by the police before?'

'No.'

'We are going to record this interview and it will be added to the formal investigation. Are you okay for us to do this?'

'Yes. Is there anything I need to know specifically before we begin?'

Luke had a lot of questions. Like why did you refer me to the same group as one of your other clients? Were you trying to fob me off because talking about my dead wife is getting boring for you? Why have you put me in the middle of this almighty mess?

But he simply turned to Hana and waited for her to answer.

'As and when we have a suspect and we go to court, the court may dictate that you release all of your records pertaining to Evie Glover. The interview we are about to conduct today is an informal one. Usually this type of inquiry would not allow a therapist to disclose personal and confidential information about a client to the police without the client's consent. However, we obviously are in an unusual situation in that respect.'

'I see.'

'I think the best course of action,' said Luke, 'is for you to provide as much context as you can and feel comfortable providing in order for us to get a better picture of Evie's life. This is how we will catch whoever killed her.'

Nicky nodded, ready to begin. He pressed the record button.

Leaning forward to note the time on his phone, he cleared his throat and began.

'It is April tenth at 7:10pm and this interview is being conducted by DCI Wiley and DS Sawatsky at the office of Dr. Nicky Bowman. Dr. Bowman, how long had you been treating Evie Glover?'

'Four weeks. I had seen her for only three sessions.'

'At any point in your sessions,' said Luke, 'did she say that she thought she might be in harm?'

Nicky hesitated just slightly, opening her mouth and waiting a moment before answering. It was such a tiny reaction that Hana, not knowing Nicky, wouldn't have caught it. But Luke did.

He leaned forward as she spoke.

'No. Evie never said that she thought she was in danger.'

'What was the general content of your sessions?' Hana asked.

'She was in deep mourning for her husband, Johnny. He had died by suicide and she was distraught.'

'What exactly did she say about her husband's death?' Hana continued, looking over at Luke.

'About Johnny's death? Well, he fell from the balcony of their flat which I understand was quite high up. She wasn't present when he died and she felt extremely guilty about not being there that evening.'

'She didn't see her husband go over the balcony?'

'No. She arrived home to police cars everywhere and at first had no idea that they were there for her husband. She talked about that exact moment throughout all three sessions with me. She couldn't get over how her life was one thing as she stepped out of her taxi and then about a minute later when a neighbour rushed over to tell her before she had even reached the building entrance, it was irrevocably changed.'

As Nicky said this, she looked directly at Luke sitting diagonally from her, as if to get across that he was not alone in his own feelings about his life pre and post-Sadie's death.

'What was the marriage like? Did you get a sense of that?' Hana asked.

Nicky took a breath and shrugged.

'Maybe a little bit. The first few sessions are usually quite specific about the event that brought the client to therapy in the first place. My sense was that there was a bit of strain in the marriage, but I don't know what precipitated that or was the cause of it.'

'Wait a second,' Luke said. 'You said that you began seeing Evie four weeks ago. Are you sure about that date?'

'Yes,' Nicky replied. 'My first session with her was March 11th and she had emailed me to make the appointment about a week prior to that. I checked the dates when you called earlier today.'

'But Evie's husband died three weeks ago. You saw her before his suicide.'

'Yes, that's correct.'

'I don't understand,' Hana said. 'She didn't come to you in order to talk about her bereavement? Then what was the event that brought her to you? Or was it, you know, general life malaise?'

'No, there was something specific that she wanted to discuss. She was having difficulty with connecting to different peer groups in her life and was feeling very alone.'

Luke was beginning to feel his irritation overtake him. He couldn't believe that he was in this situation, interviewing his own goddamn therapist about another of her clients who was brutally murdered just after he had gone out for coffee with her. A woman that he would never have met if it wasn't for Nicky.

'What on earth does that mean?' Luke said, the exasperation in his voice evident. 'Can you please be specific?'

Hana turned to look at Luke, glaring ever so slightly. She turned back to Nicky and nodded at her, hoping to encourage her to give them some sort of information that may be helpful.

'I have a particular interest in persuasive groups. I work with other therapists on a volunteer basis with individuals who have left groups like these and often have difficulty reintegrating with their old lives. And forging a new life.'

'Cults,' Hana said.

'Not necessarily,' Nicky replied. 'The term cult is quite a pejorative one. These groups are based in an offshoot of a specific religion or more focused on self-improvement, like the one that Evie was involved with.'

The instant Nicky said this, Luke and Hana looked at each other.

Lombardi had been right.

'Vision Unlimited,' Luke said.

Nicky's mouth dropped open in an involuntary movement.

'How on earth did you know that?'

They knew because Lombardi's attention to detail and the extra time she had spent walking around Evie's flat after Luke and Hana had left, soaking in everything she could see, had paid off.

She had spotted a flyer left on the table next to the condolence cards. It was emblazoned with a logo that featured the same slightly off-kilter V that had been carved into Evie's flesh.

The V was for Vision Unlimited.

Hana had done an Internet search while they were all still in the Incident Room. It was a self-improvement group, just as

Nicky had described. Its motto was *Your Vision is Unlimited. Your life can be too.*

'What the hell does that mean?' Hana had said to the room, and now again to Luke's therapist.

'It's a very basic concept,' Nicky explained. 'The group is all about self-visualization and manifesting the things that you want and the things that you feel you need to change.'

'So I can go to Vision Unlimited and visualize that I want a million pounds and the money will suddenly manifest in front of me?' Hana said, the scorn in her voice unmistakable. She couldn't bear gullible people and she couldn't bear organized religion even more. The sound of Vision Unlimited was doing her head in.

'Not exactly,' Nicky replied. 'The most common way that people fall into these groups is because they are trying to escape something else — their family, a bad relationship, drugs or alcohol sometimes — and an organization like Vision Unlimited, which seems very positive, is enticing. But these groups, and it sounds like Vision Unlimited was one of them, can quickly take over every aspect of your life so you can't make decisions without consulting them and you almost disappear overnight from the people who love you.'

'And then — let me guess — they ask you for money,' Hana said.

'This does happen, yes. But it's more about control and power — and making the participant, Evie in this case, feel powerless.'

'Was her husband part of this group as well?' Luke asked.

Nicky shook her head.

'I don't believe so. Evie said that he initially loved how she seemed like a changed person and he went along to the group for a time, but he lost interest pretty quickly. When she got more and more involved with Vision Unlimited, I'm going to guess it put a strain on the marriage and that's why she left the group.'

'I'm about to ask you an important question,' Luke said. 'Did Evie ever say to you that she thought her husband did not die by suicide?'

Nicky thought for a moment before answering.

'The only thing Evie said was that she didn't understand it. That it didn't make sense to her.'

'She never said to you that she specifically thought that her husband had been purposefully killed?'

'No.'

Hana felt a measure of disappointment at this answer. She had felt sure that they were going to be lead somewhere significant from this conversation.

'One more thing,' she said to Nicky. 'Do you know where she was staying after Johnny died? We don't believe that she was staying at home.'

'Yes, Evie said that she had stayed at the flat for the first couple of nights after Johnny died but that she couldn't bear it. Completely understandable. She then went to stay with her sister.'

Luke and Hana turned to look at each other. The unspoken moment wasn't lost on Nicky.

'What is it?'

'Nicky,' Luke said. 'Evie didn't have a sister.'

Nineteen

The man slowly slid the balcony door shut behind him, suddenly silencing the street noise of central London.

'Did you kill my husband?' Evie said to him again, as soon as the man stepped back inside the flat.

He thought her courage at this moment was remarkable.

'Does it matter?' he said. 'Johnny was a good man and now he's gone. How it happened isn't going to change anything.'

'It changes a lot for me.'

'But that's the thing about you Evie. You change on a whim. One moment we're friends, the next moment I'm the enemy. It's been tough to keep up.'

'Fuck you.'

'Well, I don't think that's necessary,' he said, as he lunged for her.

Evie was quick and he only caught her arm, which he wrenched back towards him.

She screamed and he saw that her arm was hanging limp and at a sickening angle. She gasped for breath and he pushed her into the bathroom. When she saw the bathtub running, she grabbed for Johnny's razor which was just within reach on the top of the cabinet. He knocked it out of her hand but not before she had sliced open his forearm.

'You bitch,' he hissed.

As he dragged her towards the bathtub, Evie crashed into the sink and the toothbrush cup smashed into pieces on the tile floor.

Water sloshed over the edge and the front of him was soaked as he pushed her down. He watched the blood bloom from his arm and seep into the water.

She tried to keep her eyes open underwater, blinking furiously, and he smiled.

———

He watched Evie lie on the living room floor where he had dragged her, the trail of water and blood like the slime a slug leaves behind as it moves across a pavement.

He turned her onto her back, the saliva and blood in her mouth pooling in the back of her throat where it gurgled in time with her short, raspy breath.

The last breaths she would take.

Yanking down the right hand side of her trousers by the waist, he could just reach her hip. The skin was wet and dimpled and cold. With his other hand, he struggled to pull his pocketknife out of his own trouser pocket and with one slick movement, a flick of the wrist that he had practiced since he was thirteen years old, he released the long, sharp blade of the knife.

He let the blade sink down from the tip until it had made a long enough cut, then he did the same again, creating a V. He stared at the blood that pricked out of Evie's body and then released the waist of the trousers.

With one more slow and measured movement of his hand, he sliced through Evie's jugular vein and tucked a strand of hair that had fallen in front of her eyes back behind her ear.

The man did not watch her die.

He went back into the bathroom and looked at himself in the mirror. His clothes were soaking wet and blood had smeared over his arms and hands and somehow become matted in his hair. He twisted the knob on the side of the bathtub to release the pink water down the drain. Then he pulled a fresh, fluffy towel from the granite inset shelves next to the sink and placed it on the bamboo bench that sat just outside the large two person shower.

Peeling off his clothes, he dropped them to the floor, making a neat little pile with his feet. He turned on the shower and adjusted the temperature so that it was hot and steaming. Then he stepped inside and helped himself to the shampoo on the shower shelf and the geranium body wash and scrubbed himself clean.

Towelling dry, he walked into the hallway taking a quick glance at Evie's body in the living room.

She was dead.

In Evie and Johnny's bedroom, he opened the wardrobe and moved the hangers along the rail until he found something suitable. Taking a pair of Johnny's boxer shorts out of the chest of drawers, he slipped them on and then helped himself to a t-shirt and socks, and then a pair of chinos. Back in the kitchen, he rummaged under the sink for a rubbish bag into which he placed his bloodied clothes, and he bundled it into a tight ball and shoved it into his rucksack which sat by the door next to his shoes and his jacket.

There was just one more thing to do.

He looked at Evie and smiled.

Twenty

Luke had slept terribly. This wasn't unusual when he'd had a day at work as difficult as yesterday. It hadn't helped that he'd argued with Hana as they'd left Nicky's house. He almost never argued with Hana.

The interview with Nicky had been taxing on Luke. He never in a million years thought that he would be in this situation — have to question his own therapist about another one of her clients who had been murdered.

Hana and Luke had concluded the questioning and Luke pressed the stop button on his phone to cease the recording. All three of them instantly relaxed.

'I'm sorry,' Nicky said. 'I just realized that I didn't even offer either of you some water. I was so preoccupied with trying to finish my day and get ready to see you that I forgot about it.'

'It's fine,' Hana said. 'Honestly, don't worry.'

Luke didn't know what to do with himself. Make small talk with his therapist? Stand up and leave? He looked over at Hana, slightly helplessly.

It was Nicky who ended up changing the tone of the conversation.

'While you are both here,' she said, 'it seems like an opportunity to check in.'

Luke was a bit unsure of where Nicky was going with this and Hana seemed completely lost.

'How are you both doing?'

Hana's mouth opened in a way as if to say to Luke: this is your therapist. You deal with this.

'It's been a long day, but we're fine, thanks,' Luke said, standing up and beginning to pull on his jacket.

'I know that Sadie meant so much to both of you,' Nicky said.

Hana had been halfway off the sofa, having taken Luke's cue that it was time to go, as Nicky said this and she stopped, frozen in an odd position as if she was playing a tag and freeze game in the school yard.

'What you must both be going through as you look into the circumstances surrounding Sadie's death is a lot. I know you can't discuss the specifics with me, but I am here to support you.'

Luke's limit of what he could take in today from his therapist was rapidly reaching its capacity and he simply shook his head at no one in particular and began to walk towards the office door.

'Uh, thanks,' Hana said. 'It was really lovely to finally meet you. I'm just sorry about the circumstances.'

'Me too,' Nicky said.

'We may need further details from you and will be in touch. But if anything suddenly occurs to you — any detail at all — please call one of us,' Hana said, suddenly catching herself as she said it. This was a phrase she used by rote to every witness. But now she was using it on Luke's therapist.

Hana nodded her goodbye and followed Luke, who was

already halfway down the stairs, and they made their way to their car.

'I'm happy to drop you off,' Hana said.

'It's out of your way.'

'She seems really lovely.'

'I'm going to walk, Hana. I'll see you tomorrow.'

'Luke, wait. Come on.'

In that moment, as Luke swivelled around to face her, his face betraying the emotion that he was trying to bury, Hana knew that she should just leave this alone. But she didn't.

'Nicky is right. We do need to put some time aside to go through the internet forum and figure out exactly what Sadie was involved in.'

'That's not at all what Nicky just said.'

'You know what I'm getting at, Luke.'

He whipped around and glared at her.

'We don't have time for this. Evie Glover is dead. I was the last person to see her alive, apart from her killer. Do you know the kind of responsibility I feel?'

'Yes,' Hana said, gently. 'Of course I do. But we have to find time for Sadie, too. Let's schedule an evening to go through the forum again.'

She'd pushed it too far. The second the words came out of her mouth she knew it. She had somehow, inadvertently, suggested that Luke didn't have time to look into who killed his own life. Hana looked down at her hands.

Luke took a moment to reply.

'What exactly were you doing with Philippa Nicolson last night, Hana?'

He had tossed and turned in bed all night, occasionally dropping off to sleep but only for what seemed like minutes at a time. His mind was churning over and over about Evie Glover and the sight of her dead body lying so vulnerably on her living room floor, and then of the V carved into the flesh next to her hip bone. He was thinking about his coffee with her just hours earlier, and then the bizarre interview with his therapist, and then what Hana threw out at him on the street — this comment that he should be focusing on his wife — and then, as he always did, he thought of Sadie.

As Luke stood under the steaming stream of the shower, as hot as he could stand it, he tried to shake off this unsettled feeling that had taken over his body. His appetite had left him and even the coffee he carefully made for himself once he was dressed and downstairs tasted lacklustre. He opened the fridge to see if anything at all would tempt him and then shut it again.

Luke carried his mug of coffee down the steps from the working part of the kitchen to where the enormous dining table faced out into the garden. Daffodil bulbs had finally poked out of the earth. Last spring this had made him smile, knowing that it had been Sadie, on her hands and knees, carefully digging a small hole with a trowel and pushing the bulbs down into the ground. He remembered her coming back into the house, hands muddy and a streak of dirt across her forehead where she had rubbed it, unaware it was there.

'I really hope I planted them the right way up,' she had joked.

And when spring came last year and the daffodils emerged, he told her aloud that they had in the way that he still spoke to his wife as if she was alive.

But this year as Luke stood at the window and looked out onto her daffodils, he felt only sadness. Another spring that Sadie was not here and she would not be here for every spring thereafter.

Luke walked back up to the kitchen sink, poured his coffee

down the drain and grabbed his jacket. He was meeting Hana and Lombardi at the head office of Vision Unlimited first thing when they opened and he wished that he felt more curious about the organization.

There was one niggling thing that was still rattling around his head from his conversation with Hana the previous evening on the street outside his therapist's house.

After she had deflected any talk of what she was doing having dinner with Philippa Nicolson, she threw out a question.

It was an excellent question and Luke knew that they had to figure out the answer.

'Your therapist seemed thrown when we told her that Evie didn't have a sister. Why would Evie so specifically tell Nicky this? She quite specifically told you as well. I just don't get it. Why say that you're staying with your sister if you don't have one? I mean, it feels like a stretch of a lie. I don't have a sister and I would have no idea how to pretend that I did in order to throw someone off the trail. I'd just say that I was staying with a friend.'

Although he didn't reply to Hana last night, instead turning away from her and walking home, the question had lingered. Hana was right. It didn't make sense.

Twenty-One

'I must have walked by this place a hundred times,' Lombardi said.

She and Hana were standing outside a nondescript building at the top end of Charing Cross Road, wedged between a bookshop and a fried chicken restaurant, although 'restaurant' might be a loose term. There was no sign out front, only the number of the building and a buzzer with the same V logo that Lombardi had spotted on the flyer in Evie's flat the day before.

Luke had the same reaction when he arrived to join them.

'This is the place?' he said, staring up at the building from the pavement.

It was early and the tourists who usually crowded this street were still enjoying their full English at their hotel, leaving only those Londoners who were slightly late for work, takeaway coffee in hand, manoeuvring around Luke who blocked their path. From above, it would have looked like ants funnelling around the obstacle in their way.

'Seems so,' said Hana. 'Ready?'

She pushed the buzzer and the light next to the little camera lens above it flashed on.

'Good morning, yes?' said a polite female voice.

Hana pulled out her identification and held it in front of the lens.

'DS Sawatsky from the Metropolitan Police. We have an enquiry that we believe you can assist us with. May we enter, please?'

There was a brief pause and then the door buzzed where Lombardi was ready and waiting to open it. A long, narrow staircase led the three of them upstairs where they were faced with another locked door.

'It's like the Met in here with this security,' muttered Hana, as she knocked on the door more loudly than was necessary.

The door swung open to reveal a pretty woman, probably around forty five, with a set of gleaming white teeth that were on full display.

'Hi,' she said. 'I'm Lauren. You are so welcome here.'

Hana turned to Luke and threw him a look that said she was not going to be responsible for her actions. Lauren didn't wait for any response and walked down the hall into the back of the building and Luke, Hana and Lombardi followed.

The room they were led into was a large, empty space that contained only a dozen chairs that would have looked more at home in a hotel banquet room. The chairs were set up in a semi-circle and faced one large, plush armchair, as if whoever sat in that chair was in charge.

Lauren made herself at home in the plush chair, tucking her feet up underneath herself in a cross-legged position and it was only then that they noticed she wasn't wearing any shoes. Lauren gestured for the three of them to take a seat in the semi-circle of chairs. Luke immediately knew that this wasn't going to go well.

As Luke sat down, he looked around and tried to picture Evie sitting here, which came naturally to him as he could see her sitting across from him just two days earlier at the group counselling session, her smile trying to encourage him. The emotion began to rise in his chest as he thought about her and he wasn't going to leave this room without any answers.

'Do you know a woman named Evie Glover?' he asked.

'Evie? Yes, I know her.'

'When was the last time you saw her?'

'Evie was here last week,' Lauren said.

Luke and Hana weren't expecting that answer.

'We were under the impression that Evie had left Vision Unlimited.'

Lauren cocked her head to the side and flashed her teeth at them once more.

'You never leave Vision Unlimited,' she said. 'What you learn here and what you experience stays with you forever.'

Luke did not dare look over at Hana as Lauren said this, but heard her loud and clear when she replied.

'Come again?'

'I'd be very happy to explain everything that we do here at Vision Unlimited and invite you to experience a new way of living.'

'I think just the very basics will do, thanks,' Hana said. 'So Evie attended this building regularly for your...what...do you have meetings?'

'We do.'

'And Evie attended a meeting last week?'

For the first time, Lauren hesitated and all three of them noticed it. Her smile suddenly wasn't covering for her very well.

'Evie was here, but she was just saying hello. Not attending a meeting.'

'Do you know why?' Luke asked.

'It's extremely sad,' Lauren replied. 'But her husband had just died.'

'And did you know her husband?' Hana asked.

'No, I'm afraid not.'

Luke and Hana knew that Lauren was lying. Nicky had told them the evening before that Johnny had originally come to Vision Unlimited with Evie, but had left, slightly disillusioned with it all.

'How long ago did Evie first come to Vision Unlimited?' Lombardi piped up.

'Gosh, I'd say about two or three years ago.'

'Were you here at that time?' Lombardi continued. 'Do you happen to remember the reason for Evie coming here for the first time?'

The smile was flashed at the detectives once again.

'So many things bring so many people to us. People who feel like they are lacking something in their personal or professional life. People who know that they are not achieving what they are truly capable of accomplishing. People who may have a vision for themselves, but when they look in the mirror, that vision is not reflected back at them.'

Lauren looked directly at Hana and spoke again.

'We can help you with all of that. Does any of this sound familiar to you?'

Hana opened her mouth and then abruptly closed it again. She turned towards Luke and whispered.

'Are you fucking kidding me with this?'

Luke reached over and placed his hand on Hana's arm as if to simultaneously say: I'm sorry about last night, I know this woman is crazy, and I will take over from here.

The quiet of the building was punctured by the sound of something dropping onto a hard floor. The detectives and Lombardi stopped moving as they listened intently to where the sound came from and Lauren didn't have any reaction at all.

'Is there someone else here?' Hana said, not waiting for an answer and rising out of her chair and striding towards the door.

'I - I'm not sure,' Lauren said, turning to watch Hana walk out of the door as if she could will her to stop in her tracks.

Hana looked left and right, guessed that the noise had come from further inside the building and turned left. Striding down the hallway, she suddenly slammed into the chest of a man who had just walked out of another room.

The collision made Hana cry out and Luke and Lombardi were up and out of their own chairs instantly and they rushed down the hallway to join her. Hana stepped back and took in the figure in front of her.

He was tall and broad, with a beard that would have suited both an East London hipster and a Canadian lumberjack.

All that's missing is the plaid shirt, Hana thought.

'Metropolitan Police,' Hana said curtly. 'Your name, please?'

'What's going on?' the man said.

Hana took a closer look at him. A fresh scratch was just visible at the top of his beard, snaking up towards his ear.

'We have some questions about Evie Glover. What is your name and do you know her?'

The man shoved his hands into his pockets.

'Yeah, I know her. My name is Ron Cable.'

'How do you know Evie?' Luke said, standing very straight so as to measure up to the big man in front of him. Luke was tall, but he didn't quite reach this guy's height.

Ron shrugged.

'She's a member of our community. Everybody knows Evie.'

Lombardi was just about to ask as to the last time Ron saw

her, but suddenly changed her mind.

'Do you know where we would be able to find Evie? We need to speak to her.'

Hana and Luke said nothing but both detectives were immensely impressed with this line of questioning. They understood what Lombardi was trying to ascertain.

'She's not at home?'

'We just tried there,' Lombardi lied. 'No one answered.'

'You could try Zara?' Ron shrugged.

'Who's Zara?' asked Hana.

From behind everyone came the sound of Lauren clearing her throat. As they all whipped around, the stare that Lauren was giving Ron over their heads was unmistakable. It said: *shut up*.

Ron pursed his lips and thought about his answer.

'Zara Byrd. She's tight with Evie. Evie might be at her place. Did you know that Evie's husband died? That's probably why she's not at home.'

Luke took a good look at this guy again. Something didn't feel right.

Either he was oblivious to Evie's death and was answering truthfully, or he was playing along. He was toying with them. Was he deflecting by giving them another name?

'We need the address, please,' said Lombardi.

'Sure.'

Ron scrolled through his phone until he found what he was looking for and held the screen out in front of Lombardi. She took a photo of it.

After obtaining the details of both Lauren and Ron, the detectives and Lombardi headed back towards the front door, all of them silently grateful to escape the vision of Vision Unlimited. As they were leaving, Ron called out to them.

'Detectives. If Evie calls or stops by, we'll be sure to let you know.'

Twenty-Two

Luke sent Lombardi back to the Serious Crime Unit to begin to run background checks on Lauren and Ron and anything else they could find on the members of Vision Unlimited.

Hana was just glad to be out of there. The address for Zara Byrd was in Peckham, south London and she looked at the street on her phone GPS.

'How far is it?' Luke asked.

'Not that far. She's right by Queen's Road station. It would be actually faster to take the train.'

Luke shook his head. They never knew when they had to get to their next destination quickly and to be stranded without a vehicle could be a disaster. And he was planning on apologizing to Hana — something that was always easier to do when one of them was occupied by driving through diabolical London traffic.

'Do you want to drive?' Luke asked.

'We'll get there a hell of a lot faster if I do.'

As they weaved their way through London, Hana tried to fill the silence and the tension in the car by talking about a range of subjects, jumping from one to another. Evie Glover, the cult they just left, the weather, the cafe next to the office that stopped stocking poppyseed bagels. Anything to avoid discussing their conversation the previous evening.

'Hana,' Luke finally said. 'I'm sorry.'

He chose a moment they were stopped at a traffic light to say this, and Hana felt forced to turn to face him and then apologize herself.

'I overstepped last night, Luke. I should be the one apologizing. It must have been extremely weird for you — to be interviewing your own therapist — and then she was trying to be supportive and she is the only other person who knows that Sadie was killed and I shouldn't have then pushed you on it. We'll get to it when we get to it. There's a lot going on.'

'The light's green.'

'Oh shit, sorry,' Hana said, taking her foot off the brake, but not before the car behind her beeped his horn. She waved an apology and flashed the lights on the patrol car. He backed right off.

'I hope you can understand that part of me is terrified to find out why Sadie died. And I feel responsible.'

'What do you mean?' Hana said, jerking the car into the right lane, speeding by a row of cars at a standstill.

'How did I not know what she was up to? We spent our evenings together — I mean, when I wasn't with you and working. She was sitting next to me, on her laptop, talking to people in this crime Internet forum, trying to do what I do for an actual living. I mean, it's mad.'

'Surely you can understand that I feel the same way, Luke. I have the same job as you. Sadie was one of my closest friends. She didn't tell me either.'

Luke had never thought of this. Now he felt especially useless.

'Look,' Hana continued. 'Let's deal with today and Evie

Glover. Then let's find some time of an evening and go through the forum together and get to the bottom of it. Deal?'

Luke didn't even need to reply. Of course it was a deal. He didn't say anything at all because he had no words that would be adequate enough to tell Hana how grateful he was to her.

———

Zara Byrd's block of flats was unappealing, to put it mildly. Where the interesting buildings in Peckham had been repurposed and renovated into equally interesting flats, this building had not. It would have been hastily constructed in the 1950s and looked pretty close to how it would have looked back then — ugly and utilitarian.

As they stood outside, Luke's phone rang. It was Sharma.

'Sir? We've been able to get the data back on Evie's bank card. I thought you'd want to know that for the past two weeks, she was tapping in and out of Queen's Road Peckham Station. That looks unusual with the previous six months of her travel data on the card. I haven't gone back any further than that as yet.'

'You're bang on time with that information, Sharma. Well done.'

Ending the call, Luke told Hana what Sharma had just passed along.

'So Zara Byrd is the mysterious sister,' said Hana.

'It would appear so.'

They pressed the bell for Flat 16 and waited.

No answer.

A young man pushed the front door to the building and brushed past them. Luke called after him and asked if he knew Zara Byrd.

'Yeah, she's my neighbour. You just missed her. Always

gets a coffee and breakfast at the place down the road past the station.'

Luke and Hana didn't waste a second before beginning to run back to the car. Hana didn't bother to get in, continuing to sprint down the road towards the high street, knowing that Luke would catch up with her and thanking herself that she had put time in at the gym earlier in the week. She was quick and if she was out of breath by the time she reached the coffee shop, she hid it well.

Bursting into the shop, the entire place turned to gawp at her. She scanned the customers — too many young women to be able to determine which one was Zara, if she was even here at all.

'Zara Byrd?' Hana called out.

A petite blonde woman sitting by the window looked around at everyone and then slowly raised her hand, as if she was slightly shy about answering a question in class.

'You're Zara Byrd?' Hana said, approaching her.

The woman nodded.

'Sorry everyone. Everything is fine. Apologies,' Hana said aloud, before pulling out the chair across from Zara Byrd and sitting down.

Zara looked utterly bewildered.

Aware that everyone was still staring at them, Hana desperately didn't want to create more of a scene than she already had.

'Hi Zara. I'm so sorry about that. Got a bit carried away. I just really needed to find you. My name is Hana, I'm a detective sergeant with the Metropolitan Police. I'm going to put my identification on the table here,' Hana reached into her pocket, 'so you can see it. Okay?'

As she slid the ID over, Zara barely glanced at it. She was staring wide-eyed at Hana and then around at the rest of the shop. As the other customers slowly went back to their coffees and their own conversations, Zara finally spoke.

'I'm sorry. What is going on? How did you know I was here?'

'We went to your flat and your neighbour told us. I need to warn you that my partner is about to pull up outside in our car and then come in to join us. His name is Detective Chief Inspector Luke Wiley.'

Zara now began to look frantic, staring out the window and then around the shop and then back at Hana.

'What is going on?'

Hana could see Luke parking right outside and thought about her options.

'One second,' she said to Zara, jumping up and reaching over the barista station to take a paper takeaway cup. Returning to the table, she picked up Zara's coffee and decanted it into the paper cup and handed it back to her.

'I'm sorry to interrupt your morning, Zara, but this will just take a second and we may have a bit more privacy if we step outside. Okay?'

'Sure, okay,' said Zara, still looking baffled. She picked up her puffer jacket that was hung over the back of her chair and Hana picked up her coffee for her and they headed outside to join Luke.

'Do I need to get in the car?' Zara asked, anxiously.

'No, no,' Hana replied. 'This is DCI Wiley. Wiley, this is Zara Byrd. I'm afraid I rather made a scene bursting into the shop, so we've stepped outside to have our chat.'

'Good morning, Zara,' said Luke. 'Thanks for this — we've been looking for you.'

'I don't understand...' Zara said, her sentence trailing off.

'We're here because of Evie Glover. We just wanted to ask you a few questions.'

The relief on Zara's face was clear.

'Oh,' she said. 'Johnny. The whole thing has been a nightmare. So difficult for Evie. What do you need to know? We were all so shocked that he did this.'

Luke and Hana realized that Zara had no idea that Evie was dead.

'No,' Hana said, as gently but as firmly as she thought appropriate. 'We're not here to speak to you about Johnny. We are here because Evie Glover is dead.'

Zara's face went a shade of white that the detectives did not see all that often. It happened almost instantly. Luke knew what was coming next and he lunged forward to catch Zara as she fell to the ground.

Twenty-Three

Zara Byrd was in shock.

Luke eased her into the backseat of the car while Hana went back inside the shop to buy a bottle of water and a hot cup of tea with lots of sugar.

'We're going to take you home and we can speak there, okay?' Luke said.

Zara nodded.

By the time they got her home, which took a good ten minutes longer than they would have wanted thanks to the traffic on the high street, Zara had begun to sob. It was the kind of uncontrollable crying that only the most intense emotion can invoke, and it would take some time to subside.

Hana felt absolutely dreadful for her.

She had been expecting to find this interview difficult, not wanting to engage with someone who was deeply involved in Vision Unlimited. Hana did not need her vision examined or questioned or expanded.

But all of that went out the window the moment they told Zara that Evie was dead. This was a woman stripped of everything except pure grief.

There is a particular empathy that kicked in for Luke after this had happened to him. He, too, felt extreme sadness and concern for the crying woman in front of them.

Zara's flat belied the exterior of the building. It was painted a warm maple colour and was full of a variety of lush, green plants and cozy furnishings. Hana and Luke could immediately understand how comforting this space would have been for Evie Glover after her husband had died — it felt warm and safe.

'I don't understand,' Zara stuttered through tears. 'Why would someone do this?'

'We're really hoping that you can help us answer that,' Luke said. 'Can we talk through some things with you?'

Zara seemed to be partly in another state, thinking about something else, but she nodded.

'We understand that Evie has been staying with you? How long has she been here?'

It was as if Zara realized all of the sudden that she was being questioned and that her answers were paramount to her friend. She sat upright, took a sip of water and blew her nose before answering.

'Johnny died on March 23rd. Evie called me the next day. I went and stayed with her that night — her mother was completely useless and left as soon as I got there. Then the day after that she came to stay with me.'

'Why do you say that her mother was useless?'

'She was always very prickly. Never got along that well with Evie. Her daughter's husband had just killed himself and she didn't seem to have much sympathy. She was there when I arrived and left shortly afterwards. I haven't seen her again. Does she know that Evie is dead?'

'Yes, we have spoken to her.'

'Okay. What did she say?'

'She was very upset, as you can imagine,' Hana replied.

Zara took another sip of water.

'The next very obvious question we have, Zara, is do you know of anyone who may have wanted to harm Evie? Did she mention anything to you that may have indicated she thought she may be in harm?'

Zara shook her head.

'No. We just really talked about Johnny. It was all so sad. She was devastated.'

Hana asked her next about the state of Evie and Johnny's marriage — often it's the best friend who hears the true detail of a relationship and Hana hoped that she would be forthcoming. But what Zara explained seemed very normal.

Evie and Johnny had been married for almost five years. They adored each other and after both of them had been through a string of other relationships, this one seemed to be a perfect match. It was like they had meant to be together but the timing had never been right.

'Had they known each other before they were in a romantic relationship, then?' Hana asked.

Zara paused as if she was gathering her thoughts, and then she began to cry again.

'Yes,' she was almost whispering now. 'We all knew each other at university. Drifted apart, reunited, you know, as you do when you grow up and your lives change. Some people moved away, some people had kids, the usual. But Evie was special. And so was Johnny. They didn't deserve for this to happen to them.'

'Did something happen to Johnny? He took his own life. Do you know why?'

'God, I have no idea. It doesn't make any sense to me. Maybe they had debts we didn't know about? He had a stressful job. He was a solicitor.'

'And what about Evie? What did she do for work?' Luke asked.

'She wasn't working at the moment. She and Johnny were trying to get pregnant.'

Hana figured that this was as good a place as any to dive into the subject she had been avoiding.

'Vision Unlimited,' Hana said. 'I know that you and Evie were both involved with this group. Did Evie return to it because she wanted…support…in getting pregnant?'

Luke raised his eyebrows as Hana said this and made a mental note to tease her about it later.

'Look, I know that Vision Unlimited isn't everyone's cup of tea,' Zara said.

You could say that again, thought Hana.

'But it's been enormously helpful for me at a difficult time in my life and as long as you take what you need from it and don't really bother with the rest, it's a lovely group of people to be involved with. I was the one who introduced Evie to it, and she came for awhile — and Johnny did too — but they left Vision Unlimited awhile ago. Evie only came back with me last week. I think it was nice for her to see some old, friendly faces.'

'Do you know Ron Cable from the group?' Luke asked.

Zara hesitated just slightly.

'Uh, yes. I know him.'

'What can you tell us about Ron?

'What do you want to know? He's been a member of the group for a long time. He knew Evie.'

Luke thought this was an odd detail to volunteer. Zara had been distraught for the past thirty minutes and struggling to answer their questions.

'How long had he known her?' Hana asked, picking up on the detail as well.

'A few years.'

Zara blew her nose and didn't offer anything else about Ron Cable. Luke could see Hana pull out her phone and begin to type out a text. He knew without seeing it that she was relaying this information to Sharma and asking for a full background check.

'I'm sorry to ask this,' Zara said, 'but I need to go to Evie and Johnny's flat.'

'Why?' Luke frowned at her.

'She has my keys. And I have someone coming to stay with me so I'm going to need them. I'm sorry — it's just that this building doesn't allow additional keys to be cut. Security issues. I'm going to need my set back from her.'

'We can arrange for them to be delivered to you. It's no problem,' Hana said, still engrossed in her text.

'No. I'd really like to get them myself. I know exactly what they look like. And…I guess I'd just like to be able to help. I was just in her flat. I'll know if something is out of place. Can I please try to help you?'

Luke and Hana looked at each other. It couldn't hurt.

'Okay,' said Luke. 'We'll need to arrange it and ensure that our Forensics Team is finished, but we can probably take you there later this afternoon.'

'Thanks,' Zara said.

The detectives stood up to leave, knowing they would now have more time to continue interviewing Zara later in the day.

'We'll call you,' Hana said.

'Okay.'

Luke and Hana had barely shut the door behind them before Zara picked up her phone to make a call of her own.

Twenty-Four

Lombardi and Sharma were deep into data analysis. As Lombardi cross referenced names with places of work and searched through their police files for any hint that they may have been in the system or have any connection with an existing record, she wondered if actually she was better suited to this kind of work.

She had been promoted to Detective Constable, and had been so pleased — her parents especially proud when she told them — and in the interview with both O'Donnell and the Human Resources panel she had spoken with vigour about her desire for fieldwork. But spending yesterday morning, quite literally, in the gore of Evie Glover, she worried that she was actually ill-suited for some of the gruesome work.

And she was disappointed in herself for not feeling stronger. Had Luke and Hana not sent her back to begin mining all of this data with Sharma, she might have volunteered to do so.

'Anything?' she called over to Sharma.

'I'm a little distracted.'

Lombardi watched Sharma hunched over both of his

laptop screens. One of his hands had been gripped around his metal thermos of water for at least half an hour and he hadn't picked it up once to take a drink.

'God help your chiropractor,' she said.

'What?'

'Look at you. You're like a little gremlin hunched over your computers like that.'

'A gremlin?' Sharma grinned at her.

'Well, I don't know what a gremlin is exactly, but you get the picture.'

Sharma stretched his arms back and arched his back.

'Better?' he said, standing up and placing his feet squarely on the floor and then bending down into downward dog.

Lombardi laughed.

'Okay, okay. I get the point.'

'You know, you have little concentration quirks too,' Sharma said, shifting position into a triangle pose.

'I do not.'

'Oh no? I'll take a quick photo the next time you're doing it.'

Lombardi could feel the heat rising in her neck and spreading into her cheeks. Oh god, was she blushing?

'I have no idea what you're talking about,' she tried to bluster, looking down at her laptop.

Sharma got onto his knees and beckoned for Lombardi to come and join him. He patted the floor next to him.

'Come on.'

'I'm not really a yoga person.'

'Not possible. Everyone is a yoga person. They just don't know it yet. Did you know that DCI Wiley goes to yoga?'

'You're kidding.'

'Every Thursday evening. He told me.'

Lombardi felt a pang of jealousy that Sharma had bonded with DCI Wiley in this way. Was she bonding with anyone at work? Was she being noticed? Hiding away in the Incident Room because she was too overwhelmed by a murder scene wasn't going to help.

She looked over at Sharma who patted the floor next to him again and smiled at her. It was a slightly lopsided smile and it was very cute.

'Oh, alright. But be gentle with me. I'm not very flexible.'

'I bet you're about to surprise yourself.'

Lombardi shut her laptop lid and went over to where Sharma was kneeling and joined him.

'Like this?'

'See? Doesn't that feel better already?'

Lombardi rolled her eyes.

'Okay, what now?'

Sharma leaned over and scooted behind her, gently grasping both of her forearms and pulling them down towards her calves.

'Okay, now grab your legs as far back towards your ankles as you can and stretch back. Watch.'

Sharma arched his back by pressing his chest out as far as he could and eased into camel pose.

'Gremlins, be gone!' he groaned as he felt the stretch in his body.

Lombardi giggled and tried to do the same. She had to admit that the pose felt incredible and she was relaxing on the spot.

Neither of them saw Rowdy at the door.

She watched them for a good couple of minutes before she cleared her throat.

Lombardi toppled onto her side from a low lunge. Sharma barely held his pose before jumping up and standing to attention.

'I am not even going to ask,' Rowdy said.

'Sorry, Ma'am. Stretching,' Lombardi replied, scrambling off the floor.

'I am not here to supervise. But let's see where you are. I expect Wiley and Sawatsky will be back any minute. Did anything come through on Ron Cable?'

'Yes,' said Lombardi. 'An unsavoury guy. A bit unusual that he's now part of Vision Unlimited.'

'A cult is a cult,' said Sharma. 'God knows who they attract, Joy.'

Lombardi wondered if she was warm because of the yoga or because Sharma had just used her first name. She hadn't known that he even knew what it was.

'Well, Ron Cable has been in prison for assault — both common and grievous bodily harm — and he was charged with unlawful imprisonment but those charges seem to have been dropped.'

'When was that and what were the circumstances?' Rowdy asked.

'That file seems to be sealed. I don't have the security clearance to pull it,' Lombardi said.

'Email it over to me. I'll work my magic. Sharma, Forensics said that they have sent through the initial findings.'

'Yes, I'm in the middle of going through everything and scanning it against any old cases. You never know. That's why I was distracted,' Sharma said sheepishly to Lombardi.

'Let me know if you get a hit.'

Just as Rowdy said this, Sharma's laptop made a chirping cricket noise.

'What the hell is that?' Lombardi said.

'We've got something. It's my alert if something from Evie Glover's flat pops up anywhere else on the Serious Crime Unit system. I thought I'd start there and then widen out the search.'

Sharma went over to his station and sat down, pulling

himself towards one of his laptops and clicking through a series of screens. The gremlin pose had returned.

'What the...' he said, to no one in particular.

'What do you have?' Lombardi asked, moving next to him to look over his shoulder.

Rowdy was very still as she waited to hear what Sharma had found.

'You're going to need to get DCI Wiley and DS Sawatsky here right now. We weren't expecting this.'

Twenty-Five

The man was nursing a pint. It was the kind of spring day that warranted sitting outside the pub instead of in it.

Although he didn't live in this area of London, he was drinking his beer close to Evie and Johnny's flat. He didn't usually do this — linger around the place he kills, but he knew that someone from Evie's life would be making a visit. He wanted to see how long it took and he wanted to see who it would be.

As he watches everyone saunter by him on the pavement, he sees two young men, just old enough to grow a proper beard, perhaps in their first year of living away from home. Just old enough to have fledged from the nest.

Something tugs at him as he watches the boys — their arms around each other sharing a joke, their faces to the sun.

He experienced this years ago.

It was the best time of his life.

Life at home at been miserable. His stepbrother made sure of it.

Peter was bigger than him and pushed him around whenever he could. It was as if he had been given permission by his parents — his mother who had married the man's father — to treat him the way they treated him.

To feel abandoned by your own parents was difficult enough, but Peter made it his life's mission to make it a thousand times worse. It was a painfully lonely existence in that house. And the very worst times were at the cottage they holidayed in up at the lakes.

The man was just a boy of eleven when he visited the cottage for the first time, along with his sister, who Peter seemed to leave alone. Their parents must have been there as well, but the man can't remember them being present. All he remembers is going swimming with his sister and Peter and Peter grabbing his legs from underneath the water and tugging him down. Holding him down until his chest burned and the panic forced him to take a breath.

Lungfuls of water. Choking. Unable to breathe.

And then Peter would let him go and he desperately flapped his arms up and up to get to the surface. Deep breaths of air. The panic subsiding. The tears beginning to form as he began to swim to shore.

Except Peter was right behind him. He was pulled down into the depths of the lake again.

The sound of his stepbrother laughing as he finally made it onto dry land, this game having repeated itself over and over until he gave up. Until he just wanted to die. It was easier.

He was eleven years old and shivering in his bed later that night, not from cold but from fear. He had nearly drowned and no one saw. No one cared.

He would eventually tell his sister, just one year younger than him, who would comfort him and tell him to be smarter.

Don't go in the water. Don't go anywhere where Peter is. We will get out of here eventually.

But eventually seems like a long way away and as the years

ticked by, his fear became something else. It grew and changed into something more palpable. It felt like something he could now control, instead of it controlling him.

And Peter wasn't around anymore.

He had made sure of that.

When he had become old enough to fledge that nest that he despised, with a useless father and a bitch of a stepmother, he had felt free. He had become the young man he watched now with his arm around a new best friend, their faces raised to the sun.

University had been a new world and he had felt intoxicated by the freedom and friendships. His new best friend had had a very different childhood, but they were inseparable.

Yet the fear that had grown into something else was also there. It was always there.

Twenty-Six

Lombardi was waiting for Hana and Luke at the lift.

'What do you have?' Luke asked, before the doors were even fully opened.

'I think we need to formally interview Ron Cable, first of all. But that's not what Sharma has found. You need to see it.'

When Luke and Hana entered the Incident Room, Sharma was no longer at his laptop, but pacing the room. They knew that whatever he had found had to be important because O'Donnell had joined them. He was sitting down, sipping a coffee.

Rowdy shook her head quickly at the detectives as they came in and took their coats off, signalling that O'Donnell had not yet been told about the new evidence.

Luke silently thanked Sharma and Lombardi for having the wits to not divulge this before he and Hana had seen it. It would be easier to manage this way.

'Sharma,' said Luke. 'Let's have it.'

Without a word, Sharma returned to his laptop and mirrored fingerprint images up on the screen at the front of the room.

'There were several sets of fingerprints that Forensics picked up in the Glover flat. Evie, Johnny, the cleaning lady, and two others. We know which ones are Johnny's because his prints were taken for formal identification when his body was recovered from outside the building when he jumped from the balcony three weeks ago. They are pretty much everywhere throughout the flat, but they are not on the bathtub and the shower. The cleaning lady had been through since he died.'

'And you now have an ID on the two other sets of fingerprints,' Hana said.

'No. It's Johnny's fingerprints that are interesting. No one had run them through the crime database.'

Luke could feel his chest loosening, as it always did when he knew they were just about to catch a break.

'Where did they pop up?' Luke asked.

'Here.'

Sharma pressed his keyboard and the image that filled the screen made everyone flinch.

A woman was lying face down on what looked like a tiled floor. Her eyes were open and she had clearly been dead for a couple of days when the photograph was taken. The blood was mostly dried, but it had pooled and was thick and brown and had begun to form a crust.

'Who is this?' Hana asked.

'Karen Rockland.'

'That's not possible,' said Rowdy. 'I know the Rockland case.'

'Why?' Lombardi turned to her.

'Because we have Karen Rockland's killer. DI Hackett brought him in. It was the neighbour. He was arrested just after she was murdered — a month ago.'

'You've got to be kidding me,' Hana said, reflecting what everyone in the room was thinking.

Luke walked up to the screen as if getting a closer look at

Karen Rockland's dead body was going to make this puzzle clearer.

'Let me get this straight,' Luke said. 'Johnny Glover's fingerprints were at the scene of Karen Rockland's death.'

'That's correct, Sir,' replied Sharma.

'And the neighbour — were his prints found in Johnny and Evie Glover's flat?'

'No, Sir. But one of the fingerprint sets from Evie and Johnny's flat was also in Karen Rockland's home. Unidentified.'

'Jesus Christ,' Luke said.

'What are you thinking?' Hana asked him. 'Tag team murder and the neighbour is innocent?'

Luke didn't know how to answer this. It would be the most likely explanation.

'Sir?'

'Yes, Sharma. What?'

Sharma cleared his throat, but it sounded more like a nervous tic than trying to muster attention. He already had that.

'This isn't what I thought you should see.'

'There's more?'

'Yes.'

Once again Sharma brought up an image on the screen, but it didn't look like much — a photograph of one of Karen Rockland's injuries.

'What is this?'

'I just thought it was very strange that Johnny Glover's fingerprints would turn up at another crime scene. I mean, we weren't even looking at him. He's not a suspect — he was dead before his wife was murdered. But when they popped up, I looked through the entire forensic report on Karen Rockland's body. It said that she had some small cuts and abrasions and I zoomed in to take a look and...well...'

Sharma zoomed into the image, enlarging it on the screen and everyone saw it at the exact same time.

On Karen Rockland's hip, about an inch to the left, was a small incision that would have been made by a sharp blade. The figure of a V, with a single line in front of it.

'Oh my god,' said Hana.

Luke's hand flew up to his mouth and he turned to look at her.

'It's not a V on Evie Glover. It's a Roman numeral. It's a number five. Karen Rockland is number four.'

Twenty-Seven

The room was silent for a moment. Sharma and Lombardi were astounded at the depravity of the act. This killer had carved a running tally into these women.

For Luke and Hana, as chilling as this was, they were both suddenly feeling overwhelmed by the much larger task in front of them. Serial killers were a different animal to catch.

'We should have considered this before,' Luke said.

'What? That the cut was a number on the victim? Come on, Luke. It made more sense that it was a V for Vision Unlimited,' Hana replied.

As the detectives argued about this, Lombardi felt herself shrinking inside. This mistake was because of her. It was her mistake.

'I'm sorry,' she stammered. 'I just saw the flyer in Evie's flat and I thought...'

'There's been no mistake, Lombardi. Don't sweat it,' Hana said to her. 'There is something going on with that group and they do need to be investigated. What more do we have on Ron Cable?'

'Rowdy is pulling the file,' Lombardi said.

Hana nodded and turned back to look at the image on the screen. She swore under her breath.

This son of a bitch, she thought. *We're going to get you.*

———

Detective Inspector Hackett was having an early lunch at the cafe down the street from the Met, when Luke and Hana walked through the door. He waved to them and motioned to join him but as they walked towards his table, he could tell instantly from the look on their faces that something was wrong. The paper napkin that he had tucked into his collar to protect his white shirt from the messy burger he was in the middle of eating suddenly seemed very silly. He pulled it out as the detectives reached him and he wiped his hands.

Both Luke and Hana liked Hackett — he was a salt of the earth kind of detective. He got into policing for the right reasons, which you couldn't say about everyone. He was thorough and kind with the families of victims and, importantly, also intensely disliked Detective Superintendent Stephen O'Donnell.

Hackett was one of the only work colleagues that Luke invited to the small drinks reception after Sadie's funeral, held in the bar of a private member's club to which his late wife belonged. Luke remembered how Hackett put his arm around Luke's shoulder and just held it there as they drank their wine. No words were going to suffice and no words at that time were necessary and Hackett sensed this.

He glanced down at his half eaten burger as Luke and Hana slid into the booth opposite him.

'What's wrong?' he said.

'Sorry to interrupt your lunch, Hackett. I know you're

trying to get a moment of peace from the seventh floor, but we have something that's urgent,' Luke said.

'It's the Karen Rockland case,' Hana added.

'What about it?'

'Evie Glover, the woman found murdered in her flat yesterday. We've had prints back from the scene and there are two sets of individual fingerprints that are a match to ones found at Karen Rockland's flat.'

'That's impossible.'

Luke shook his head.

'I'm afraid not.'

'We arrested the next door neighbour for Karen's homicide.'

'Any chance we're wrong?' Luke asked.

Hackett leaned back and rubbed his face with his hands, like he hadn't slept in days.

'There's always a chance we can be wrong,' he said.

This is why Luke admired Hackett — sometimes it was hard to find a detective of his rank with this kind of humility.

'Do you want to talk us through it?' Hana asked.

Hackett pushed his half eaten burger aside, no longer hungry. He jerked his head towards the waiter who came over, pad at the ready to take Luke and Hana's order.

Luke asked for a Diet Coke. Hana asked for the club sandwich, extra mayonnaise. Both men looked at her in awe.

'What? I'm really hungry. Go ahead, Hackett. Tell us what we need to know.'

Hackett detailed what they saw when they entered the house. Karen Rockland's body had been lying there for almost three days. It had been her work that couldn't reach her, and then her parents, and then any friends and a welfare check had been performed by officers.

It had been an unholy mess. Clearly a struggle had ensued and there were smashed objects in both the living room and kitchen. She was wearing only a bathrobe and had been stabbed several times. There was no evidence of a sexual assault. There had been no sign of forced entry.

At these last two details, Hana and Luke knew that Hackett and his team had the wrong guy.

'You picked up the neighbour quite quickly. Why?'

'The flat had been attempted to be cleaned by the killer. Lots of bleach, cleaning products, what have you. The empty bleach bottles were found buried in the neighbour's rubbish bin. Forensics also picked up a few of his prints still in the flat.'

'Along with two other unidentified sets of prints,' Luke said.

'More than two, actually.'

'How did he get in?'

'He had a key to both her front door and back patio door. The guy swore that he had forgotten he had them — they were in a drawer in his kitchen — and said that the previous tenant there had given him the set in case of emergency but he never used them.'

'How long had Karen Rockland lived in the flat?' Hana asked.

'Two months.'

'And how did the neighbour explain his prints in the flat?'

'He said they were old — he had been in the flat a few weeks earlier when he dropped off some Amazon packages that he had signed for. He stayed for a cup of tea, apparently.'

'But you assumed that he had been watching her and then killed her. Was there any other motive?'

At this question, Hackett was quiet. Luke could tell that he was spinning every detail about this case over and over in his head.

'If you have other forensic evidence that we have this wrong, then we'll re-examine everything,' Hackett said.

Hana's club sandwich had arrived and she quickly checked

her phone before reaching for the ketchup on the table. Hackett and Luke watched her read whatever was on her screen and then slowly lower the bottle back onto the table. She looked up at Hackett.

'I think we just found exactly what you're looking for.'

Twenty-Eight

Dr. Chung had taken the lift up to the seventh floor from the bowels of the building where she usually spent her day. She seldom came up there, preferring to leave the detectives to their work and interpreting her first analysis without any interference.

But for some reason, Evie Glover was different. She wanted to deliver this news in person.

She had printed out a copy of the report and shoved it into a manila folder and made her way upstairs to share it with everyone herself.

The Serious Crime Unit was quiet and Dr. Chung wasn't sure if this was normal or not. She prayed that she wouldn't run into O'Donnell, but peering down the hall she could see that his office was empty.

She did know that although Laura Rowdy had her own office right next to the one occupied by DCI Wiley, she rarely used it. Rowdy preferred to pace the halls, be on top of what everyone was doing, only darting into her office for a private phone call or to look at something on her computer.

Dr. Chung stood halfway down the hall and scanned for

any sighting of the diminutive woman that everyone was ever so slightly intimidated by, but she did not see her. As she made her way towards the Incident Room, she was surprised to see Rowdy sitting, quite formally, at her desk.

'Laura?'

'Oh, hi Dr. Chung, what can I do for you?'

'I don't usually see you sitting in here.'

'And your presence doesn't usually grace the seventh floor.'

Dr. Chung smiled and walked into the room.

'Take a pew,' Rowdy said, pointing to the chair in front of her desk.

Dr. Chung sat down and looked around the room. Large filing cabinets were stacked higher than was probably regulation and lined two of the three walls of the office. Rowdy was more analogue than digital when it came to certain things, and she was probably the only person who would be able to find anything with ease in her elaborate filing system. There were no adornments in the office, except for one. A simple framed photograph of a young boy, around twelve years old, smiling at the camera and holding a small trophy.

Rowdy caught Dr. Chung looking at it, picked it up and handed it to her. This gesture was strangely touching, and Dr. Chung accepted the frame carefully.

'Did you know I have a son?' Rowdy said.

'I didn't actually.'

'You have two daughters, yes?'

Dr. Chung nodded.

'It is tough sometimes. This job and having kids. It can wear on you.'

'How old is your son?'

'He's old now. Off and living his own life. Thank god.'

'My daughters aren't quite there yet.'

'They will be, Dr. Chung. And you'll know that you did a good job.'

Dr. Chung couldn't help but sigh. She smiled at Rowdy.

'And how will I know that?'

'Because you will never have taken your job home with you and your daughters will be very proud of you even though they don't have an actual clue about how hard our days are.'

In this moment, Dr. Chung had felt more grateful to a colleague than she had done in quite some time. She quietly thanked Rowdy.

'In the meantime,' Rowdy said. 'It appears that we have missed something with Evie Glover. Forensics have come back and fingerprints in her flat were also lifted from a homicide that occurred a month ago.'

'Karen Rockland. I know.'

Rowdy was very still.

'What do you have?' she asked.

Dr. Chung opened the manila folder and slid the report over the desk. Rowdy began to read and then looked up at her.

'This was found in both women?'

'Yes. Minuscule, but it's there. Fibres found in the wounds of both women. The wounds that composed the Roman numerals. And we also have the tests back on them. The wounds were ante mortal.'

'Meaning that Evie and Karen were both alive when the killer carved them?'

'Yes. And there is something on the blade that has left these fibres. It's unusual.'

'Luke and Hana need to see this.'

'I've emailed everyone already. I just — I just wanted to make sure that the team had it and understood it right away.'

'Dr. Chung,' Rowdy said. 'We understand. And we understand why you're up here.'

The team would be assembling momentarily now that Luke and Hana had this information. Rowdy had been looking at her own file. And she'd had to do some digging to pull it out of the part of the Met database that was easily buried and forgotten. Except this file had been forgotten on purpose.

Ron Cable had been arrested for unlawful kidnapping, the charges then dropped and he was released. Usually the complainant name was left attached to the file. Minds could always be changed later in some situations and it was good to keep the record. But this name had been redacted. Rowdy couldn't imagine why.

She flipped the case file to the front page and looked for the name of the investigating officer. It practically jumped off the page at her.

Detective Philippa Nicolson.

This was either going to be tricky or lucky — and Rowdy was about to find out.

She stood up and walked to the door of her office, closed it and leaned against it as she scrolled through her phone and dialled. Philippa answered straight away.

'Laura.'

'Good afternoon, Philippa. I didn't think I'd be speaking to you twice in a week, but the week has rather called for it.'

'What's happening?'

Rowdy decided not to give her a rundown of what had happened to Evie Glover, or to Karen Rockland, and see what Philippa would say about this file. The one thing she didn't wonder is if Philippa would remember this specific case. Philippa never forgot a detail.

'I'm hoping you can help the team with something. An old arrest has popped up in a background check and while the charges were dropped, the name of the complainant has also been redacted. It's a little strange. The suspect arrested was Ron Cable — just before you retired. The charge was unlawful kidnapping.'

There was a brief beat of silence on the phone before Philippa confirmed that she remembered the case — and she remembered the woman who had gone to the police and then recanted her story.

'She was scared and she wanted to disappear. I felt it was best to let her do that.'

'I'm going to need a name, Philippa.'

Twenty-Nine

The man had taken the patio key to Karen's flat five days before he planned to kill her. They had been out at dinner and when she left the table to use the washroom, she had also left her purse behind. He had to guess at which key to take, but figured that the slightly smaller one he took was the patio door key.

He never had plans to go skiing that weekend.

He had expected Karen to be out for the evening with friends and imagined that he was going to have a few hours to be in her flat, think about what he was going to do, and prepare. He had only been in the flat once before.

The man hadn't seen Karen come home from work, but when he hopped over the wall from her neighbour's garden, he saw her through the glass wall that separated the garden from the kitchen. She was pouring a glass of red wine and pulling out little containers of food from a tote bag.

Then he watched her lay the fire.

She put sticks of kindling into the grate, carefully arranged at an angle, and then twisted up pieces of newspaper very tightly and lay them on top. He saw her pick up the box of matches from the bookshelf and then put it down again.

She was going to do something else before she lit the fire. And then she left the room.

He waited a minute, and then another, and then quickly moved over to the patio door, inserted her key into the lock and tried the handle. It turned easily and he let himself in.

The shower was running.

This excited him. She was already in the bathroom where he had planned to fill the tub with water. For later.

But the fireplace excited him even more.

It had been accidental, his love of fire.

He had turned thirteen years old, still ignored by his father and stepmother, still tormented by Peter. They had been up at the cottage in the lakes again.

It was a cold, dark February late afternoon.

When they were at the cottage in summer, he tried to stay outside in the woods — away from the house and away from his stepbrother. But in the winter he was forced to stay in his bedroom, away from the staircase that led down to the cellar — away from the stairs he was pushed down and then locked behind. It was cold, and dark and terrifying down there. The door locked from inside the house and try as he might, it was impossible to get out.

Even at thirteen, he was frightened of being locked in there and sometimes Peter would not release him for hours. Not until he heard the sound of their parents' car on the gravel driveway outside the cottage, returning from their frequent visits to the pub.

There were no neighbours. There was no one to call for help.

But on one February day, Peter had been forced to go down into the cellar himself. The house was freezing and the space heaters that were plugged in all over the house had blown a fuse. The house was pitched into darkness and Peter had found a flashlight and descended the steps into the cellar to find the switch to flip it back on.

He watched Peter open the door to the cellar and disappear.

Without thinking, he rushed towards it, quietly closed it and turned the lock.

And then he smelt the acrid smell of something burning.

The lights flashed back on and he could see that a fire had started in the living room. The heater beneath the window had set fire to the curtains.

He stood there in awe of the flames that licked the fabric and were shooting up to the ceiling.

Peter had tried to open the door. He couldn't.

Peter had sworn and shouted for his brother to open it. He did not.

The thirteen year old boy listened to the sound of his brother's nails scraping against the door, searching for a handle, a lock, anything that would release him.

He watched the fire spill into the room.

Thirty

Rowdy had come up with a name for their missing woman connected to Ron Cable, whose name had been redacted from the unlawful imprisonment charge. And she really was missing — there was no record of her. No driver's license, no bank cards, no address.

There was always a moment in the middle of a case when Luke felt overwhelmed. He knew that it would pass but right now there were too many threads to this case and not enough leads and he didn't like it.

Everyone was assembled in the Incident Room and Hana had taken over the white board. She was scribbling on it in columns and her handwriting was illegible and it really wasn't helping.

'What the hell does any of this say?'

Hana spun around and glared at him.

'Hana, you really need to stick to typing.'

She turned to Sharma and pointed at the board with her pen.

'Sharma, what does this say?'

Sharma looked frozen on the spot by the question. He opened to his mouth to attempt to answer and then declined.

'Sorry, DI Sawatsky. I actually have no idea.'

'Oh for god's sake all of you,' Hana muttered. 'Fine — Lombardi, start typing as we go through everything. You can mirror it up here.'

The identical fibres in the wounds on the two women had given them definitive evidence that the same killer was involved in both cases, and likely with the same weapon.

'The biggest question in front of us at the moment is: why was Johnny Glover at the scene of Karen Rockland's murder? He clearly didn't kill his own wife, but did he kill Karen? How was he involved?'

'That's three questions,' Hana said.

'Helpful, thank you,' Luke shot back.

Dr. Chung, who had waited around to make sure the team had the fibre evidence was sitting on a chair by the coffee machine.

'Is it always like this?' she asked Lombardi.

'Yep, pretty much.'

Luke instructed Sharma to dig into Johnny Glover and find out as much as he could.

'We need to get to know this guy,' Luke said. 'And we don't have a lot of time. Two killings in one month. Let's not think about what might be about to happen. We won't let it. So while a full psychological workup would be nice, I'd rather you focus on anyone we can actually talk to who knew this guy.'

'Well, Zara would have known him,' Lombardi said.

'Yes. Why don't you come along to Evie Glover's flat this afternoon. Forensics are done there now and I've let Zara know that we would meet her outside the building in,' Luke checked his watch, 'about 45 minutes.'

Zara was nervously checking her phone when the three detectives pulled up to the Glover's building on City Road. When she saw them approaching, she didn't move to greet them, standing frozen to the spot.

Luke had the feeling that this was going to be difficult. The woman was probably still in shock, in the first stages of profound grief, and about to walk into her dead friend's home.

As they took the lift up to the fourteenth floor, everyone was silent. Hana unlocked the door to the flat but turned to address Zara before she opened it.

'It's important, even though the Forensics Team has completed their sweep in there, that you don't touch anything. If you want to move anything, please ask us first.'

Zara nodded.

Luke and Hana felt for her. Walking back in somewhere for the first time since that person has died is always so difficult and Zara was doing this for the second time. First Johnny, and now Evie.

'There also has not been a full clear up in here, so you may find the sight of blood distressing.'

Hana stepped through the door first and walked into the living room. The other three followed her and if Zara was shocked by the sight of the flat, she did not display it.

'When was the last time you were in here?' Hana asked.

'Just after Johnny died. She called me and I came over the day after it happened. Police were here that day, too. I didn't speak to them though.'

'That would have been a welfare check by our support officers,' Luke said.

'Do you know where your keys might be?' Hana asked.

'No. Do you mind if I look around? I won't touch anything.'

Zara crossed her arms in front of her, as if to show the detectives that she understood their instructions and she began to look around the room. She was staring at the surfaces and down on the floor. The blood stains were dark and had likely seeped into the hardwood panels.

'Does anything seem out of place to you, apart from what would have been created by the disturbance before Evie was killed?' Luke asked.

'Not really,' Zara said.

'What about Johnny's things?' Lombardi suddenly piped up. 'Is there anything specific to Johnny in this flat that seems odd to you?'

'What do you mean?' Zara said, her voice sounding tight.

'We are beginning to wonder if the two deaths are connected,' Hana said.

Zara looked taken aback by this comment, and then collected herself.

'I — I don't know. I'll see if anything stands out. I'm going to keep looking around, okay?'

Zara continued to walk around the flat and the detectives noticed her constantly turning to look at the balcony. When Lombardi caught her eye, she stopped moving around the flat and took a breath.

'Sorry, I just can't imagine Johnny going over the balcony. I felt the same when I came over just after he died. I don't know how Evie could stand being back here. I wish she'd never come back. She should have just stayed with me.'

After another five minutes of going through the flat, the keys had not been located and Zara didn't think she saw anything that was particularly out of the ordinary, beyond the obvious.

'I'm sorry, I need to use the washroom,' she said.

The detectives hesitated, knowing that she would have to touch surfaces in order to use the toilet and wash her hands.

'Fine,' Luke said, and Zara excused herself and shut the bathroom door behind her.

As the detectives waited, they spoke in lowered voices about their next move — which was difficult to determine at this point. Their best bet at the moment was that Sharma was going to come up with something on Johnny, or that they would find the woman who had accused Ron Cable of abducting her.

Lombardi thought she heard something and looked up at Luke and Hana to see if they had heard it too. They hadn't reacted, still deep into their conversation about the forensic evidence. Lombardi moved closer to the bathroom door and strained to hear what was happening inside. There was the very faint sound of items being moved — maybe in the mirrored cabinet? Lombardi had her ear as close to the door as possible without touching it. There was silence and then she heard the toilet flush and the sink tap turn on.

Stepping back, she waited for Zara to emerge and as the door opened, she thought she saw Zara tugging her sleeve down over her wrist and holding it there with the tips of her fingers.

'All done, thanks,' Zara said, moving past her.

In the lift on the way back down to the lobby, Lombardi stared at Zara's sleeve. Was she imagining it or was there a slight bulge in it? Her fingers were still tugging the sleeve down and holding it firmly closed. Was she hiding something?

She had been wrong about the V symbol and the logo on the Vision Unlimited flyer. She didn't want to say something to Wiley and Sawatsky and be wrong again. Her fieldwork days, whether or not she felt she was cut out for it or not, could be numbered if she led them down another wrong path.

In the lobby, Hana put her hand on Zara's back and expressed her condolences again.

'Thank you,' Zara said.

Luke nodded his head towards Lombardi and for a split second she felt relief that he, too, had noticed that Zara might have taken something from the flat. But then she remembered that she had been asked along on this excursion to speak to Zara about Johnny Glover.

'Zara,' she said. 'Can we ask you a couple of questions about Johnny.' There was no inflection in her voice, as she hoped that her tone would elicit a useful answer and let the detectives know that she was taking this line of questioning seriously.

Zara stopped short on the pavement, having already begun to walk away from the detectives and back towards the tube station.

'Um, sure. What would you like to know?'

'Well, for starters, what did he do in his spare time?'

'His spare time? Honestly, I have no idea. We weren't really close at all. Evie was my friend. He was, you know, the husband appendage.'

She laughed then, and covered her mouth with her free hand as she did so, a tick so common in self-conscious children that was usually outgrown by adulthood.

'Did he have any hobbies? Any particular group of friends?' Lombardi asked.

Zara shrugged her shoulders.

'I think he liked playing snooker. He used to go somewhere to do that.'

Luke and Hana exchanged a look and Lombardi caught it. She wasn't doing a very good job. Maybe the detectives were making Zara a bit nervous, or maybe she was just really shit at this.

'Thank you, Zara,' Luke said. 'We'll be in touch if we need

anything else and you have the Met support officers number should you want to speak to them.'

'Yes, thank you.'

Lombardi was feeling a bit frantic, wondering what she should be doing here.

'Are you heading to the tube station?' she asked Zara, in desperation.

'Yes.'

'Great,' Lombardi said. 'I'll walk you up there.'

A last ditch attempt to get some useful information.

Luke and Hana got into their car to head back to the Met and Lombardi and Zara walked up City Road towards the station. The day was even more springlike as the afternoon wore on and the two women engaged in small talk.

Neither of them saw the man just a few paces behind them.

He had been sitting outside the building in the sunshine after finishing his pint. His timing had been fortunate to spot the detectives head inside. They hadn't stayed long in there.

He was particularly surprised to see Zara with them. He hadn't expected that.

Thirty-One

Lombardi stood outside Angel tube station. Her interview subject had long disappeared into the cavernous underground and was probably miles away by now on the train.

She didn't quite know what to do. The thought of heading back to the Met without any intel on Johnny Glover felt like a massive failure as the thought of trawling through data with Sharma, cross-referencing names and addresses and dates, seemed equally disappointing.

She decided to call into the Incident Room and see if anything else was needed. She was patched through to Hana's mobile, as the detectives weren't quite back yet and Hana suggested that she return to Vision Unlimited and see if she could gather any information from Ron Cable.'

'Nothing heavy handed,' Hana warned. 'Just background. How long has he been with the group, where does he live, how well did he know Evie Glover, did he know her husband?'

'Basically just background?'

'Yes. He may inadvertently give information that he's not

aware he's giving you — and that will begin to fill in some gaps for us here.'

'Okay. Got it.'

Relieved to be able to redeem herself, Lombardi saw a bus with Trafalgar Square as its terminus approaching and hopped on it.

The man who had been following her the entire way from the flat building tapped his card on the reader right after her.

———

Bobby Sharma had just completed the equivalent of a 1000 piece jigsaw puzzle, mostly comprising pieces of the same shape and the same colour. And he'd done so in under two hours. He was ecstatic.

When he hung up the phone with the final piece of information he needed, he raised his arms aloft in victory and looked over at Lombardi's empty chair. He wished she'd been here to see him pull this off. She'd know about it shortly, of course, but in this job it was the small moments where everything clicked that you wanted to share with someone. Before you knew it, everyone was racing to the next thing and the moment was forgotten. But Sharma guessed that you could pretty much sum life up that way, too.

When Sawatsky and Wiley arrived back, he was still grinning.

'Oh god, what have you done?' Luke asked him.

'You're going be extremely pleased.'

'Let's see. What is it?'

Their missing woman. Lisa Toby. She was on her way into Scotland Yard to speak with them.

'You're kidding,' Hana said. 'Are you sure it's our girl?'

'Oh I'm sure. She seemed eager to come in.'

Luke walked over and slapped Sharma on the back. A hug

would have been too much, although he had considered it for a split second.

'How the hell did you pull this one off?'

Sharma had been waiting for them to ask this.

How do you find a woman who has seemingly disappeared? You think about her frame of mind at the time — why would you do this and what would you do next?

'I'd probably be leaving the country,' said Hana.

'Well, yes,' said Sharma. 'That was our one stroke of luck. If she had, it would have been referred to Interpol and you know how messy that can get. But if you didn't leave the country, what would you do? I'd want a fresh start. Somewhere away from London but not too far. And what is better than a fresh start than enrolling in school?'

'You did a college and university search.'

'I did. I figured if she wanted her name kept off that record, that meant that she wasn't changing her name. And I found her — a bursary was applied for and granted, in association with a loan, at the University of Surrey.'

'Sharma, you genius.'

'Oh, it gets better,' he said.

Sharma described how he pieced together his elaborate jigsaw puzzle. There was still a loan amount due for Lisa Toby, and it was being paid off in monthly increments, so Sharma felt it was a good chance that the corresponding details for the account would be correct. He received an address in Kent from the university and that address did not have a landline, but there was an associated mobile phone number. When Sharma called it, he found Lisa Toby's mother. She did not want to give out her daughter's information, but instead took Sharma's details and within thirty minutes, his phone rang and it was Lisa Toby on the other end of the line.

'She just called you back?' Hana said.

'Yep. I did not give out any information about our current

case. Or should I say cases? I asked if she would be willing to speak to DCI Wiley and DS Sawatsky and I didn't have to ask twice. She offered to come in. She's on her way.'

Luke picked up the espresso cup into which he'd just made a coffee, and took a sip.

'Any idea why she's so keen to speak to us?'

'No, Sir. But you've got to think that it's a good sign.'

'A good sign for the case,' Hana replied, 'but maybe not a good sign in terms of what it means.'

Thirty-Two

It had been an exhausting day.

Lombardi had started and ended it at Vision Unlimited and she was glad to get the hell out of there. Everyone she spoke to was odd and creepy. The whole place gave her the creeps.

Twice now today, the buzzer was answered by Lauren and she was welcomed warmly into the building. Without Luke and Hana backing her up, Lombardi found herself being interviewed by Lauren and she wasn't sure how that happened.

What did she like about herself? Why did she think that was? What did she envision for her future? What was holding her back in achieving it?

The question racing through Lombardi's mind during all of this was: how did I find myself on the back foot here and how do I stop it?

She stopped it by requesting to speak to Ron Cable.

'You've just missed him, I'm afraid.'

Lombardi wasn't buying it, so asking, not very politely, to look around, she stood up and began to stride towards the back of the building where they had run into him before.

She got to the door that she guessed he had come out of that morning and she grasped the door handle. It was locked.

But she could see someone in there, their shadow moving just slightly through the frosted glass sliver that ran down the left hand side of the door. Lombardi rapped loudly.

'Metropolitan Police. Open the door.'

The shadow stopped moving, and as if acknowledging that he had been caught, flicked the lock. Lombardi heard it slide back but the shadow did not open the door for her. She wondered briefly if he had a weapon and was waiting for her.

Glancing back down the hall she had just walked down, she was surprised to not see Lauren following her. In fact, she couldn't see or hear anyone else. The sinking feeling in her stomach that she had been purposely left alone made her wonder if she was in danger. She looked back down the hall again and thought of running. Getting the hell out of there.

But she was being ridiculous. It was only just dark, the team knew she was here, and she had a job to do.

Lombardi grabbed the door handle and pushed into the room.

Ron Cable was standing there, smirking at her.

It took her a moment to figure out what this room was for — it seemed part kitchenette and part office. Lombardi noted immediately that there was no exit.

'Cup of tea?' he said to her, his upper lip curling as he spoke.

Lombardi stared hard at him.

'No. Thank you.'

'And what can I do for you?'

'Just a few questions if you don't mind.'

'I do mind. But I suppose you're not going to take no for an answer, are you.'

Lombardi began to question him — all background infor-

A Spirit in the Dark 179

mation, just as Luke and Hana had instructed. She had felt stupid pulling out her notepad and pen, so instead she held her phone behind her back and pressed the record button. She would transcribe it later when she got home and send in the report.

Lombardi thanked Ron for his time and slipped her phone into her pocket. She'd turn off the recording once she was out of the building so as not to draw attention to the fact she had done so.

As she turned to head back into the hallway, Ron called after her.

'Miss Lombardi was it? I hope you get home safely.'

She didn't turn around, getting the hell out of there as quickly as possible.

There was no point in stopping by the unit on her way home — it was the wrong direction for one thing, and if anyone from the Serious Crime Unit needed her, they would call. Lombardi was tired and she wanted to transcribe this interview and get it off to Sharma and then put on a baggy sweatshirt and make a bowl of pasta. And sleep — she could really use some sleep.

Two buses later, and a ten minute walk, she was home.

She unlocked the front door and called out for her flatmate. There was no answer and Lombardi said a silent prayer that she had the house to herself. She washed her hands and her stomach growled. Pasta first, then transcription.

As she busied herself in the kitchen, pouring water into a pot and looking through the cupboards for a jar of sauce that wasn't expired, she was unaware of the figure standing right outside her front door.

The man was staring at the lock and considering his options. He walked back to the pavement and looked up at the windows, smiling at the lack of street lighting and the large hedge that blocked the house from the road.

He'd be back.

Thirty-Three

'Thank you so much for coming in,' Luke said.

He and Hana had met Lisa Toby in his office, instead of a formal interview room. If she was brave enough to come in to speak to them, they needed to make her feel as comfortable as possible.

Luke's office was ordered and calm. Hana always teased him that it was like being in his house. Apart from the basic Metropolitan Police furnishings, he had a comfortable arm chair in the corner. The chair was a Scandinavian design with large, felt cushions and thin wooden legs. He knew that his colleagues teased him about it behind his back — and sometimes in front of it — but he had the chair for three reasons. Although he rarely sat in it himself, he liked to look at it from his desk and be reminded that there was life outside of the stone and brick walls of New Scotland Yard and that it was a life that could be beautiful and carefully chosen and curated. He liked to be able to offer it to someone who perhaps needed to be handled delicately, as was the situation with Lisa Toby at this moment. And he loved the chair because his wife had bought it for him for the first two reasons.

When he had left the Met a year and a half ago after Sadie died, Hana had arranged for the chair to be moved back to Luke's London house, although she noticed that it remained in the alcove of the front vestibule, and never moved any further inside. She suspected that everything that had happened with the Marcus Wright case and the mistakes Luke had made at that time were things he didn't want to think about and so didn't want anything associated with the Met to be part of his home.

But when Luke decided to come back to work a little over a year later, Hana popped into his office one morning with bagels and a coffee (that she knew he wouldn't drink) and the armchair was back. He didn't say anything and she made no comment at all, except going over and sitting in it as she bit into her breakfast. She thought that perhaps the reason it had returned to the Met was to show his colleagues that he planned to be back at work for some time — and if anyone here knew what actually happened to Sadie and who had killed her — Luke was sticking around until he found out.

Rowdy had brought Lisa Toby onto the seventh floor, having collected her in the lobby, and straight to Luke's office where he and Hana were waiting.

She was in her late twenties, tall, with long blonde hair. If they had been worried about her willingness to be there, they were soon reassured as she strode confidently towards them and shook both of their hands.

It was clear that Lisa Toby had something to say.

Offers of tea or water were declined and Hana, Luke and Lisa sat in a comfortable silence for a moment before Luke began.

'We really appreciate you coming in to speak to us. I would ordinarily say in such a position that you're probably wondering why we wish to do so. But your willingness to come in makes us think that you perhaps know what this is regarding.'

Lisa rubbed her thighs and looked directly at them both.

'It's to do with Ron Cable, isn't it?'

'Yes,' Hana said. 'We are working on a case that is quite time sensitive and his name has come up. It's possible that he is not involved in any way, but when we ran a background check, we managed to pull the file about your unlawful imprisonment charge.'

'We know that you requested to keep that private,' Luke added.

'Did you speak to Detective Nicolson?' Lisa asked.

'We have.'

'She was extremely nice to me. When I wanted to drop the charges, I desperately wanted to put this behind me and for some reason I felt I could only do that if the record was wiped clean. She said she couldn't do that, but she tried to remove my name at least. She was very understanding.'

'Yes, Philippa Nicolson has the tendency to be understanding,' Luke mused.

'I think you'd better tell us the whole story,' said Hana.

'Okay. It all started with Vision Unlimited — around five or six years ago.'

Lisa Toby had been in her early twenties and as she put it "a bit lost and impressionable". She had seen an advertisement for Vision Unlimited so went along to an introductory meeting to see what it was all about.

She got sucked into it, and quickly.

'And that's where I met Ron Cable,' Lisa said. 'I thought he was so cool but I look back now and he didn't treat me very well. In fact, he was awful.'

She was quiet for a moment, looking at her hands. Hana and Luke wondered where this was going — why would she so readily come into Scotland Yard to speak to them about this guy?

'Did something happen between you two?' Hana prodded, very gently.

Luke wondered if Lisa had become emotional and was embarrassed in front of them, or if she was finding whatever she came here to say too difficult to say aloud. But she took a deep breath and raised her head and told them exactly what had happened.

'There was a guy,' she said. 'I don't remember his name. It was something common that wouldn't stick out — like Paul or David or James. He hung around the Vision Unlimited Centre quite a bit, but not because he was part of the group — he made it quite clear that he couldn't give a shit about it and thought we were all pathetic — but he was friends with people there.'

Luke and Hana's ears were standing to attention as she said this.

'Do you remember who the friends were?' Hana asked.

'Yes. He hung around with Evie and with Zara.'

Luke then made a calculated decision and one that he felt might solicit more detail from Lisa and an urgency to provide it.

'Lisa, we're very sorry to tell you that Evie is dead. She was killed and we are looking for the person who did it. This is why your information is so important to us.'

Lisa looked shocked at this revelation and the detectives could see her jaw muscles tensing and releasing.

'You think it's Ron, don't you?' she said.

'Do you feel that he would be capable of killing someone?' Luke asked.

Lisa shook her head, not to dispel how dangerous Ron might be, but to give herself time to think.

'I guess anything is possible. But what happened between

me and Ron was complicated and he was only partially to blame for what happened that night.'

'Would you like to tell us a little more about it?' Hana asked.

Lisa told them about the night. She had been hoping that Ron was going to ask her out and he had — they'd gone for drinks, but the other guy had come along, too. There had been far too many drinks and when it was suggested that they take the party back to someone's flat, she was going along. When she realized that she was alone with Ron and the other guy, she got nervous and tried to leave.

They wouldn't let her.

They held her down.

She thought she was about to be assaulted, but that wasn't what happened next.

'The guy pulled out a pocketknife and cut me with it. But not like a quick slice. He held me down and cut into my arm really carefully, like he was carving his goddamn name or something. He had done the first cut and I screamed. As he was putting the knife back in me to carve something else, Ron realized what was going on and pushed him off me. I ran for my life.'

Hana and Luke were both open mouthed as Lisa finished her story. Luke felt a rush of anger that this killer had been hunting women for so long and not only did they not have him yet, they hadn't even known he existed.

'And you went to the police,' Hana said.

'Yes. I reported what had happened, but then I got scared. And I hope you can understand that I felt bad too. I had really liked Ron and I didn't know the other guy's name but I said that it was Ron who had held me against my will. After I'd thought about it for a couple of days, I realized that I really just needed the entire thing to go away. I was scared of that psychopath finding me, I obviously wasn't ever going back to Vision Unlimited, and I just wanted to move on with my life.'

'So you went to Detective Nicolson and asked her to make it disappear.'

'Yes. But as the years have gone on, I've never forgotten what happened. I wondered if other girls were being hurt like I was and I always thought I would tell someone what really happened at some point. Then I got your call.'

'Where did this happen?' Luke asked.

'I'm not sure. I think it was at Ron's flat. I'm sorry, I honestly can't remember.'

Hana marvelled at this woman's bravery and how she had come back to the police to do the right thing.

'Lisa,' she said, 'do you know what he was carving into you?'

'See for yourself,' Lisa said, pulling up the sleeve of her jumper to show Luke and Hana two almost identical neat lines, the scar no longer raised on her skin, but still gleaming white.

Thirty-Four

Lombardi's pasta might have been the best meal she'd eaten in weeks. Or she was just really hungry. She had begun watching a movie that was on the television, one that she had seen multiple times before but it was comforting to settle into it after her trying day.

By the time the movie was finished, she really didn't feel like transcribing the interview with Ron Cable. She pulled out her phone and pressed the play button on the recording .The sound quality wasn't great, but she could hear most of it and she told herself that the transcription wouldn't take too long. She couldn't let the team down. Knowing Sharma, he was still sitting in the Incident Room, hunched over his laptops.

She left her phone on the coffee table and picked up her dinner dishes, taking them into the kitchen. She looked at the rubbish that had been collecting for several days now and that both she and her flatmate had been ignoring, hoping the other one would take it out. It was beginning to smell.

Lombardi picked up her laptop from the kitchen table and took it into the living room, opening it up and creating a new document titled Ron Cable Interview, with today's day. She pressed play on the phone and began to listen to it.

But she was now distracted by the rubbish. It was so silly — why not just take it out? Lombardi reached under the coffee table for her shoes, which were lying exactly where she'd kicked them off a little over two hours earlier and shoved her feet into them.

Once the rubbish bag was out of its bin and tied up, Lombardi opened the front door and walked towards the bins.

The man was waiting.

He grabbed Lombardi from behind and she dropped the bags. His hand was not clamped over her mouth, but she was so surprised and the adrenaline surging so quickly through her body that she did not scream.

It took her only a couple of seconds to react and her training kicked in. She swivelled and tried to break free of his grasp, but he was so much bigger and the strength of his forearm around her throat began to choke her.

She couldn't breathe.

Her feet were flailing against the pavement and she tried desperately to make noise. Any noise at all. But all she could hear was the man's heavy breathing. It was so close to her face.

Lombardi knew she had to keep fighting, but she couldn't breathe and her vision began to blur.

―――

When she had stopped moving, the man carefully carried her as far as the large hedge that blocked the front garden from the road where his van was parked. He lay her on the ground while he peered out to the pavement and checked that there was no one approaching. Luckily for him it was dark — the council clearly not spending enough money on street lights.

Then he darted to the van, opened the back, and returned

to the limp body of Joy Lombardi. He picked her up and carried her to the open door, lay her gently inside and shut the door.

Calmly, the man walked back towards the house. He left the rubbish bags where they had fallen and with his sleeve, pulled the front door shut.

He walked back to the van, climbed into the driver's seat and started the engine.

Thirty-Five

The man had never grabbed a woman like this before.
He had never killed a stranger.
But something about seeing the police woman with Zara had whet his appetite.

She had regained consciousness in the back of the van, but he had tied her up very carefully. Once he got to his house with its private garage, he knew that he could easily get her into the house without being seen.

The house he lived in had a loft extension that was never finished by the previous owner, who had run out of money. The insulation had been installed, but the plastering had never been done.

Before he had returned to the police woman's house, he had reinforced the door to the loft with planks of wood from his shed and brought in a chair and plastic wrist ties.

He was ready for her.

―――

He had thought he had been ready for Karen as well.

When he heard her shower running and saw the fire she had laid but not lit, he couldn't help himself. He took the box of matches from the fireplace where he knew she kept them from his one and only previous visit to the flat and he struck one. The man held it up in front of his face and stared at it. He watched it burn and it went out when it singed his fingers. He lit another one and this time he bent down and he lit the tightly wadded newspaper.

The fire quickly sprang to life. He could feel the heat.

He moved back into the kitchen and looked around. What could he tie her up with? He was unprepared to improvise this quickly as he thought she would be out with friends and he would have time to set up properly. He knocked the heavy metal corkscrew off the counter by accident and it clattered to the floor.

The man froze and waited.

The shower turned off.

Usually he liked to tease and play with them a little more, but he could make do.

The man pulled an old pay as you go mobile from his jacket pocket and typed out a quick text.

I know you're in there.

Karen was nearly dead. She had been unconscious for about twenty minutes and her breathing was now intermittent.

The man left her on the kitchen floor and walked down the hall into her bathroom. He pulled out a little box that contained cotton ear swabs and carried it back to the body. Pulling one out of the box, he carefully inserted the tip into the V incision he had made in her flesh, right next to her hip bone. Then he pulled out his wallet and eased out a coffee shop loyalty card that he kept there and pressed the tip of the cotton swab onto the card onto the empty space where the free coffee logo would have been stamped by the barista. The blood soaked into the paper.

The man slipped the cotton bud back into the box and then into his pocket with his wallet.

It had been a thrilling evening, but there remained one large problem. Karen had been noisier and had fought more than he had imagined she would. The man was worried that neighbours had heard.

So he called the one person he knew who would pick up the call from the old pay as you go mobile. He gave him the address of Karen's flat and waited.

Johnny arrived less than an hour later.

Good old, reliable Johnny.

The two men had not seen each other in at least a year. Once the best of friends, a bond formed at university that the man thought would never be broken, but it had fractured. Evie had got in the way.

Evie who had once been really fun, who had been introduced to him by Zara. They were the firmest of friends once upon a time, too.

But then Evie got to know him.

She didn't like how he treated women. She didn't like how he treated Johnny. She didn't like him at all. All thanks to Vision Unlimited. Before she joined that group, she had been the life of the party. She had been the one that egged him on and loved his sudden sharp tongue and his intensity. But when she got involved with that crazy group of people, she had suddenly changed her mind about him.

She gave Johnny an ultimatum. Their marriage or his friendship with his oldest university friend.

The man had the feeling that it had been a tough decision. And even though he hadn't seen Johnny in all of these months, he knew that Johnny would turn up.

He had instructed Johnny to bring bleach. They would use the cleaning products already in the house. Bless the guy — he didn't even ask why the man requested it. That was his weakness — to just do as he was told.

The man loved Johnny but he hated his weakness.

Thirty-Six

'Do you think Lisa Toby was going to be number two or number three?' Hana asked, standing in Luke's kitchen and staring in the fridge, which wasn't offering much.

It was seven o'clock in the morning and she knew that Luke wouldn't be sleeping either. This is what she had said to him when she knocked on his door ten minutes earlier.

'Just because I might be up, that doesn't necessarily mean you have to drive over here for breakfast,' Luke said.

'Fat chance of that happening,' Hana replied, closing the fridge door. 'So, what do you think about Lisa Toby?'

Luke swirled his coffee cup around, inhaling the aroma.

'Until we have another definitive victim, it's impossible to know. She could be number two, or she could be number three and Ron Cable fought him off before he could carve the third line for the Roman numeral into her.'

'Which means we still don't have number one either.'

'No. I think that Johnny might be the key to this and before we left last night, I asked Sharma to really dig into him and see what he could find that may be useful.'

As if on cue, Hana and Luke's mobiles chimed at the same time with a text message.

'Sharma,' said Hana. 'The guy is psychic.'

'No, I think he's just being extremely polite and ensuring that we are awake before he calls us.'

Luke pressed Sharma's name on his phone and connected through to him.

'Good morning, Sharma. I'm going to put you on speaker. Hana is here. No, neither of us sleep.'

'Oh, good morning DS Sawatsky.'

'Hi, what's up?'

'Actually, I couldn't sleep either, so I came into the office a little early. I wasn't finding much on Johnny Glover apart from all of the information and people we'd already talked to for background. But then I thought about the condolence cards that Evie received and began to go through them from the Forensics file. I think I have something.'

'I thought perhaps you did with this crack of dawn call,' Luke said. 'What is it?'

'One of the cards is from a Dan and the marriage certificate for Johnny and Evie is signed by a Daniel Marsh. Could be the same guy?'

'Do you have a number or an address?'

'I've got a couple — let me narrow it down and I'll send it over to you.'

'Perfect,' said Luke.

The call being finished, Luke stood up and wandered towards the fridge, pulling out a carton of eggs.

'Do you know what these are called? Eggs. You crack them open and cook them.'

'Poached, thanks,' Hana said. 'Any toast with that?'

Luke rolled his eyes and pulled out a pot from under the counter and began filling it with water.

'There are bagels in the freezer.'

The light was just beginning to filter into the loft.

Lombardi had spent the past nine hours in complete blackness. It was a claustrophobic, terrifying night. She had no sense of what time it was or how much time was passing. To calm herself down she began to count seconds into minutes and then every thirty minutes she tried to calculate how much time in total had elapsed.

It provided no comfort at all.

The light at least let her know that someone would now know she was missing. How quickly would the team put together that Ron Cable had abducted her? She imagined that it would happen very fast. He was the last person they knew she saw yesterday and he had a record for unlawful imprisonment. They would send a special response team and she would be freed, hopefully within an hour or two.

The sound of creaking stairs sent a shock of fear through her. She swallowed but there was no saliva. The plastic ties had cut into her wrists after hours of trying to wriggle free and blood was dripping into her palms.

Lombardi could hear wood being moved and lowered to the floor and the door to the loft swung open. More light than she was expecting flooded in and she squinted, desperate to see past Ron Cable and a possible escape route.

When she opened her eyes and focused on the figure, she did not recognize him. She had never seen this man before in her life.

Oh my god, she thought.

No one was coming.

Thirty-Seven

When Luke and Hana walked into the Incident Room post-breakfast, Sharma was waiting with good news. He had found the correct Daniel Marsh who had promised to call Luke as soon as he was finished his morning meeting.

'Has anyone heard from Lombardi?' Sharma asked. 'She's not picking up.'

Hana frowned. That was unusual. Lombardi was extremely punctual and was working very hard to be noticed at the moment.

'How long have you been trying her for?'

'I don't know. Almost two hours? It's weird. Even if she's working on something, she'll pick up. Did you assign her somewhere this morning?'

Luke opened the door and wandered down the hall to find Rowdy.

'Have you seen or spoken to Lombardi yet today?' he asked.

Rowdy shook her head.

'No. Why?'

'I'm sure it's nothing. She's not picking up.'

'Do you want me to send a patrol car over?'

'No, thanks, Rowdy.'

Luke returned to the Incident Room and the look on Hana's face said everything he needed to know.

'Sharma,' Luke said. 'You've been hunched over that desk for too long. Why don't you drive DS Sawatsky over to Lombardi's house and just check that everything's okay. Maybe she's not feeling well. I'd like someone to lay eyes on her.'

'Yes, Sir. But DS Sawatsky, would you prefer to drive?'

'Read my mind. Let's go.'

―――――

The rubbish bags lying on the grass of the front garden was the first thing they both noticed when they arrived at Lombardi's house.

'Does she live alone?' Hana asked.

Sharma was embarrassed to admit that he didn't know.

Hana knocked on the door and when there was no answer, she tried the handle. The door opened with ease and Sharma and Hana looked at each other in alarm.

'Lombardi, it's DS Sawatsky, are you home?'

As Sharma followed her into the house, he suddenly felt very cold. Something was not right.

'Her phone,' he said, spotting it on the coffee table in the living room.

Hana picked it up and the screen was filled with missed call notifications.

'What the hell is going on?' Hana muttered under her breath.

'Here, give it to me,' Sharma insisted, taking it out of Hana's hands and punching in Lombardi's six digit code.

Hana raised her eyebrows.

'We sit next to each other all day,' he said, in way of explanation.

The phone opened to the voice notes app and Sharma pressed play. Ron Cable's slightly muffled voice filled the room and the uneasy feeling that Hana had on the way over to Lombardi's house was quickly turning to panic.

Lombardi's laptop was open on the coffee table, but they couldn't access it.

'I think she was transcribing the interview,' Sharma said. 'And she was going to send it in. That clearly didn't happen.'

The two of them put Lombardi's phone back on the coffee table and crouched over it, listening to the interview. They heard the low, gruff voice of Ron Cable call out at the end of the recording.

'Ms. Lombardi was it? I hope you get home safely.'

Hana didn't waste a second making the call to Luke and Rowdy.

'I need the tactical team at the home of Ron Cable. Right now.'

Thirty-Eight

The tactical team was going to take twenty five minutes to get there.

Luke and Rowdy were pacing the entire seventh floor.

How could he have let this happen?

As if Rowdy knew what he was thinking she tried to reassure him.

'This isn't your fault.'

'Rowdy, I sent a very junior, newly minted Detective Constable with no fieldwork experience to interview a possibly very dangerous criminal. I'm absolutely responsible.'

'We'll get her. Don't worry.'

This might have been marginally comforting had Rowdy not looked extremely worried.

'Can you patch us into what's happening? They must be almost there. Did Hana and Sharma head over there to wait?'

'Yes, and yes. I can feed it into the Incident Room.'

Once Rowdy had the feed from the tactical team up and running, Rowdy shut the door and the two of them stood in front of the screen. They watched the team break down the front door of a council flat and move neighbours out of the way.

Luke was holding his breath. He could hear the voices of the team leader calling that room by room everything was clear. The flat was tiny. It did not take long.

'DCI Wiley,' the tactical team leader shouted into his radio. 'There's no one here.'

———

The team was stood down and Hana and Sharma were informed that Lombardi was not being held by Ron Cable. Officers were sent down to Vision Unlimited to bring him in for questioning just in case, but they doubted they were going to get very far.

Luke felt sick. Even the water he was sipping was making him feel nauseous. When his phone rang and it was an unknown number, he answered in about a millisecond.

'DCI Wiley.'

'Oh hi. I think you were trying to get in touch with me? My name is Daniel Marsh.'

Luke closed his eyes and tried to take a breath. He didn't really have time for this call right now, but he also had time to kill before Hana and Sharma returned so that he didn't go crazy.

'Yes, hello. Thanks for calling. We understand that you were the best man at Johnny Glover's wedding, is that right?'

'Yes, that's right. What is this about?'

For a second, Luke didn't know how to answer that — what was this about? Evie Glover? Her husband? Karen Rockland? The fact that one of the best colleagues he'd ever worked for had been abducted?

'We're trying to get some background on Johnny Glover.'

'Oh right. Well, I was the best man at both of his

weddings, actually.'

Luke stopped pacing.

'I'm sorry. Johnny was married twice?'

'Yes. To Evie. And before that to Zara.'

Luke desperately looked around the Incident Room for someone, but he was standing in it completely alone. He ran to the door and yanked it open, scanning the hallway for Rowdy. When she saw him running towards her, she stopped what she was doing, fear in her eyes waiting to be told something horrific.

Luke quickly shook his head once to indicate that he wasn't coming to her about Lombardi, but that he needed her listen to this call with him. He needed someone else to take in this information too.

Jamming his finger into the phone and putting the call on speaker, Luke asked Daniel Marsh to repeat himself. He affirmed once again that before Johnny was married to Evie, he was married to Zara.

Rowdy was on her own phone the second Daniel Marsh said this, calling to have officers pick up Zara Byrd immediately and bring her in. As she dealt with that arrangement, Luke wandered back into his office and sat down in his grey, felt Scandinavian armchair.

'Do you know why Johnny and Zara divorced?' Luke asked.

'Zara was difficult. She had a tricky childhood from all accounts. But the big problem was her brother. He was really off-putting, needed a lot of attention. Something was definitely wrong with him.'

'Wrong how?' said Luke.

'You know, totally charming one minute and a complete psychopath the next. But Zara adored him and Johnny did, too. Meant there were three people in the marriage. That never works out.'

Thirty-Nine

Thirteen-year-old Adam Byrd watched the flames lick the furnishings in the living room of their cottage and he was transfixed.

The sound of his stepbrother pounding on the cellar door finally broke him out of his trance and he raced up the stairs two at a time to reach Zara who was in her bedroom.

'The cottage is on fire. We have to go.'

Adam reached for Zara's hand, still so much smaller than his even though she had just turned twelve, and he pulled her towards the staircase.

'Where's Peter?' she said.

'Don't worry about Peter.'

As they reached the top of the stairs, Adam could see Peter's room to the right, and sitting on top of his bedside table was his pocketknife. He darted inside, grabbed it and slipped it into his own pocket.

Now it was his.

When they reached the ground floor, the fire had spread quickly and Zara cried out. The banging on the cellar floor was now frantic. Peter could smell the smoke and very soon he would hear the cracking of the wood beams splintering around him.

'We have to get him out,' Zara said.

Adam looked at his sister very calmly and shook his head.

Then he leaned towards the cellar door and called out to his stepbrother.

'How does it feel knowing you're about to die?'

Forty

By the time Zara was placed in the interrogation room on the seventh floor of Scotland Yard, the address of her brother, Adam Byrd, had been passed to the tactical team. They reached the house in under ten minutes.

Adam was arrested and taken directly to hospital. He had attempted to stab himself with his pocketknife when his front door was broken down by officers and it was determined that he needed a psych evaluation. The tactical team reached Joy Lombardi within the hour she hoped she would be rescued. But it was Bobby Sharma who burst through the door of Adam Byrd's house right after the tactical team, not being able to be held back by Hana. He reached her as paramedics were bandaging her wrists and insisting she lie down on the stretcher.

'Sharma,' she said, surprised and enormously relieved to see him.

He threw his arms around her and did not care how awkward this was for both of them. He couldn't imagine what he would do if something had happened to her.

'I'm sorry,' he muffled into her, not letting go.

Hana watched the two of them, thinking about herself and Luke and the bonds that this job created. There was still a lot to be done.

In the interrogation room, Luke wasn't going anywhere until he got some answers. He was going start with Zara Byrd and as he began to talk to her, his overriding emotion was one of pity.

Her brother always told her what he did, what he got up to, who he killed. She kept his secrets close and had done since she was twelve years old. She was frightened of her brother, but she loved him.

She had loved Johnny, too, who had probably loved Adam more than anybody else. He also knew about the women Adam hurt and the final straw had been Karen Rockland. When he had been roped in to help clean up Adam's mess, he could no longer live with himself. And so he didn't.

Zara's grief on the day he and Hana told her that Evie had been murdered was genuine. She had not known what Adam had done, but she knew that it was him. It had to be. She convinced herself, and she tried to convince Luke, that Adam had only killed her because he was scared that Johnny had told her what they'd done.

Luke wasn't so sure about that.

She explained that she had to get into Evie's flat to look for any evidence of a bloodied cotton swab, her own fear being that a similar one was found at Karen's. The card in Adam's wallet would have the blood evidence of both women on it.

'And what about the other victims?' Luke asked her.

'I don't know where the other girl is,' Zara replied, beginning to cry for the first time since she had been brought in and charged as an accomplice.

'But number one,' she whispered, 'is my stepbrother.'

The first little notch scratched into the shiny silver shell of the pocketknife, now safely in the hands of the Serious Crime Unit Forensic Team.

Forty-One

Luke wanted to visit Lombardi in the hospital, where she would be staying for observation for a few hours. The rest of the team was taking the afternoon off.

Hana went with him and Luke stopped in the hospital gift shop on the way. He stood in front of a shelf of plants and balloons and stuffed animals and picked up a little fluffy penguin.

'Are you serious?' Hana said.

'What? Everyone likes penguins,' he replied, paying for it at the counter.

'You don't need to feel like what happened to Lombardi is your fault,' Hana said as they rode up in the lift.

'I've already had that lecture from Rowdy, but thanks.'

'I mean it. I think you feel responsible enough for everything else.'

Luke knew that she was talking about Sadie.

When they reached Lombardi's room, they could barely see in through the throng of people who had gathered. Squeezing past everyone, Hana and Luke reached her and she seemed surprised to see them.

'Detectives,' Lombardi said, 'meet my...entire family.'

The relief that Luke suddenly felt, seeing so many people who loved Joy Lombardi surrounding her with affection, was something he hadn't felt in a long time.

'Brought you this, Lombardi,' he said, holding out the penguin.

'Oh. Thank you.'

'Everyone loves a penguin, apparently,' said Hana.

Luke and Hana left Lombardi to the care of her family and drove back towards Luke's house.

'Order in?' Luke asked.

'Vietnamese. And I want everything.'

The entire way back in the car there had been an unspoken conversation — Luke was sure that Hana also felt this. They needed to do what Hana had been urging him to, and Nicky had been in support, too.

Hana had barely finished her first prawn summer roll when Luke asked if he should get Sadie's laptop so they could look at the Armchair Investigation forum together.

'Great idea.'

'How in depth have you gone through what Sadie was posting in here?' Luke asked.

'Quite in depth. You?'

'Same.'

They knew that Sadie had been looking at around half a dozen specific crimes — mostly unsolved — and that one of these had gotten her killed.

'I think we're going to need a little bit of help from this forum to really understand what Sadie thought she discovered,' Luke said.

'And how do you want to do that?'

'I thought I'd post.'

'On the site,' Hana said, completely deadpan. 'You're the Detective Chief Inspector of the Serious Crime Unit at Scotland Yard. You can't just post on a crazy crime fan website.'

'No, but I can message someone privately through Sadie's account and explain who I am. Someone that she trusted.'

'*Dee123*,' Hana said.

Luke couldn't help but laugh.

'Exactly how much time have you been spending on this website? But yes, *Dee123*.'

The detectives had both spent hour upon hour trawling through Sadie's posts and the person she interacted with the most was a user named *Dee123*.

'So let's send her a message,' Hana said.

'Right now?'

'Why not?'

Luke had to go with the moment and take advantage of a successful day at the office, an afternoon off, and Hana's optimism. He quickly composed a message:

Dear Dee123. This is Luke, Sadie's husband. I wonder if you might have a moment to speak with me.

Luke's finger hovered over the 'Enter' button, as he wondered where this message would lead, if anywhere. It might be nothing and then they would have to start from scratch again. He pressed it.

Luke and Hana began to settle into their afternoon — their bowls of steaming noodles eaten and their phones mercifully silent. Sadie's laptop screen suddenly flashed to life, the chime of the incoming message was an unfamiliar sound.

Luke pulled the laptop towards him and clicked on the bolded, new message. It was from *Dee123*.

'Yes. We need to speak. I think something happened to Sadie.'

DCI Luke Wiley returns in

Hidden Demons

About the Author

JAYE BAILEY is a writer living in London. She is a big fan of true crime and detective fiction and the characters of Luke, Sadie and Hana have been in her head for a long time. Jaye finally decided to put pen to paper and begin the DCI Luke Wiley series.

When she's not writing, Jaye loves to travel. When at home, her house seems to be the destination house of choice for all the neighbourhood cats and, in her humble opinion, she makes the best spaghetti bolognese on the planet. (Yes, she will send you the recipe.)

Find out more at: jayebaileybooks.com

TWO
YARDS

Printed in Great Britain
by Amazon